The Green Portfolio

by G. H. Teed

Illustrated by J. H. Valda

First published in the Union Jack magazine,
Series 2, No. 1066, Dated 15 March, 1924.

Stillwoods Edition 2022

Stillwoods.Blogspot.Ca

Catalogue Information:
Title: The Green Portfolio
Author: G. H. Teed (1881-1938)
Illustrated by: J. H. Valda
First published anonymously in the Union Jack magazine, Series 2, No. 1066, Dated 15 March, 1924.
ISBN Canada: 978-1-989788-87-5
Blog: Stillwoods.Blogspot.Ca
Author Blog: http://ghteed.blogspot.com/
Storefront: http://www.lulu.com/spotlight/lulubook22

https://tinyurl.com/ve25d42s This link should go to a spreadsheet of all known Teed stories. The list is annotated with various information on the stories and my progress with recapturing the work. The library of Teed's stories increases almost weekly. Check at the Lulu.Com for the latest arrivals. Search for Teed./drf

Keywords: Sexton Blake, British fictional detective, Tinker, Japan, 1923 Earthquake, Korea.

Cautionary Note: This series of books by Stillwoods are intended to make the stories of G. H. Teed, born in New Brunswick, Canada, available to collectors and researchers. The editor, or rather digitizer has not altered the original publication.

This story may contain language and racial terms that are not appropriate to today. I apologize for them; I know that the author was using his voice to excite and entertain an adventurous English audience. These works were published from 82 to 110 years ago. Most every work has characters of redeeming ethnicity within.

I hope you enjoy and share these stories; I have.
Doug Frizzle

Introduction to this second release of 2022.

This is the second digital recovery for 2022. I have been looking at how things have come along after the disaster that Lulu.Com created in 2020, and which took me near a full year to recoup. The disaster was prompted by the withdrawal of Adobe Flash player upon which all of Lulu's web pages were based.

I notice that there are quite a number of Teed novels that never did make it back into the fully 'published' columns of my spreadsheet. That is to say they are not available from Barnes and Nobel, and Amazon—they are strictly available from Lulu.Com.

I notice further that there is no 'Author Spotlight', a feature web page that describes my purpose in this hobby.

Supposedly one can order and search within 'My Publications' web page. This feature seems sporadic, for whatever reason.

I do notice that there are very few 'Teed' publications within Lulu.Com—so that is the best way to locate these old works. Go to Lulu.Com and search on 'Teed'.

I believe that the lowest prices are on the Lulu.Com site. Checking Amazon just now shows a significant difference in price—twice as expensive on Amazon—Canadian site!

With the release of this story, over 5 million words by Teed are published in 162 stories. Note that a number of stories are available only in web page format—about 40, mostly 'Nelson Lee' novels.

There are still quite a few, over 50 stories in my archives which have yet to be digitized. I do have another life which frequently has to be serviced!

Anyhow, please enjoy! If you have questions, FrizzleDR@gmail.com will get to me.

Doug   Stillwoods

Some of the latest works in progress or published at **Lulu.Com**

The Pirated Cargo
The Grey Domino
The Sweater's Punishment
The Great Cigarette Mystery
Black Sea Sailor –Solovyev
The Beggar in the Harem –Solovyev
The Enchanted Prince –Solovyev
The Green Portfolio
A Soldier and a Man
At the Turn of the Hour
The Sunken Schooner
The Black Emperor
The Idol's Spell
Dead Man's Rock –Q
The Adventure of the Giant Bean
Rosalie –Day
Victory Garden –Day
John Paul's Rock –Day
The Curse of the Cardews –W M Graydon
Ghosts of the Spanish Main –Dell
The House of Curtains

Several pages (8 of 28) of this issue are not available, the pages of 'The Detective Supplement.'

CAN YOU BEAT IT?-NO!

A Long Complete Story of SEXTON BLAKE, TINKER, AND HUXTON RYMER and the GREAT JAPANESE EARTHQUAKE.

An earthquake—a dead body—and something stolen from a pocket! That's how the thing began. It was Huxton Rymer who stole it, and that fact accounts for the astonishing events which followed. This yarn tells of Rymer's one big chance to "clean up" a gigantic fortune— and how he was coolly frustrated by Sexton Blake of Baker Street.

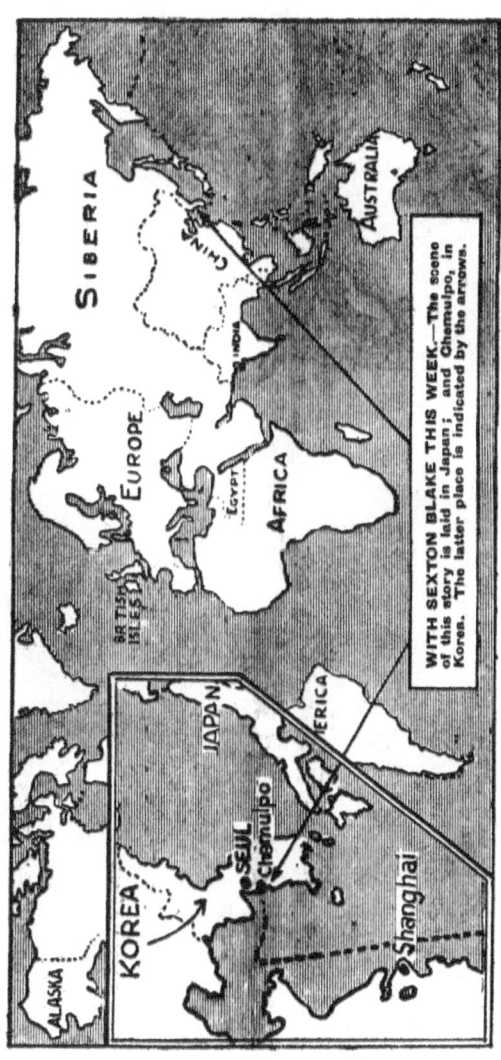

WITH SEXTON BLAKE THIS WEEK.—The scene of this story is laid in Japan; and Chemulpo, in Korea. The latter place is indicated by the arrows.

THE GREEN PORTFOLIO

A Story of the Great Japanese Earthquake—and of Huxton Rymer, Adventurer.

Pictures by J H Valda

An earthquake—a dead body—and something stolen from a pocket! That's how the thing began. It was Huxton Rymer who stole it, and that fact accounts for the astonishing events which followed. This yarn tells of Rymer's one big chance to "clean up" a gigantic fortune—and how he was coolly frustrated by Sexton Blake of Baker Street.

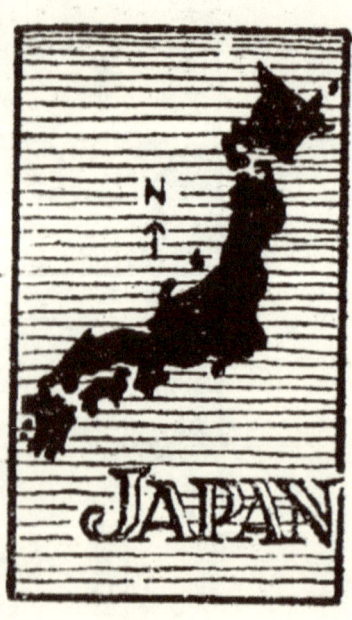

The First Chapter.   Death and Destruction.

WHEN the recent great earthquake picked up one corner of the southern island that forms the larger part of Japan, and shook it as a terrier would a rat, there broke loose, as is always the case in such disasters, all the evil passions of men which terror can let loose. There is not a single upheaval, or great fire, or flood, on record where such has not been the case.

It was the same during the Johnstown disaster. There was looting and murder, and worse, at the time 'Frisco was destroyed. The same evil passions were unlocked in Jamaica when Kingston tumbled like a cardboard town that sunny afternoon a few years ago. A few shipwrecks have been free of such scenes, but there are others whose horrors are best forgotten.

So it was in Japan, and far, far worse than the outside world has been allowed to know, if one might judge from private letters which have come through since, by way of Hong Kong and Manila. The Japanese themselves revealed many fine traits of character, when all they owned in the world was being devoured by that ghastly holocaust. But, unfortunately, in their very midst was a colony of fierce Koreans, who seized the opportunity to spread across the stricken area, committing every outrage that their savage minds could conceive.

As is known, the Japanese, the foreign colonies of British and Americans, and the crews of foreign ships in port at the time, made heroic efforts at salvage and life-saving. But their efforts to control the panic were as nothing compared to the wave of outrage which swept from Tokio to Yokohama when the Koreans and thousands of convicts broke loose.

To describe one of those terrible scenes is to describe them all, for the gangs roamed aimlessly about the roads beyond reach of the devouring flames, seeking their victims anywhere among the fleeing refugees.

Some of them were of short duration, some of them developed into miniature battles, but none of them raged more fiercely than one which broke out just in front of what had been the Grand Hotel, on the bund at Yokohama, and in which two burly Europeans might have been seen taking part.

These two men, one of medium height but stocky, with heavy

shoulder muscles bulging beneath his white drill coat, had all the earmarks of a coast skipper; the other, taller, with pointed black beard scarcely concealing a strong, sweeping lower jaw, and with shoulders even more powerful than those of his companion, had been seated sipping long, cooling drinks on the back veranda of the Grand when the first tremor had been felt.

Both men had felt the sinister tremble of an earthquake before, and they wasted no time in "getting from under," so to say.

With one accord they came to their feet, and, just as the second and more violent shock rippled beneath them and seemed to lift the building bodily from the ground, they rushed to the door of the adjoining dining-room, where a crowd of recently landed tourists were at tiffin, and shouted a warning. It was scarcely necessary, for already the panic-stricken crowd was making a rush for the doors.

For a few minutes the scene that followed was terrible.

Women were shrieking with terror, children, affected by the sweep of panic but not understanding what it meant, joined their shrill treble cries to those of their elders. Men were trying to keep a way clear to the doors for the women and children to escape, although a few, with the green of deadly fear showing, had made an attempt to dash through in advance.

It was then that the two men who had been sipping drinks on the veranda came into action,

A simultaneous growl rumbled in the throat of each as he witnessed this arrant craven cowardice, and their heavy fists began to drive out as regularly as if they had been steel pistons, the while they chanted that age-old cry of the sea when a noble ship is going to her doom: "Women and children first—you cowardly dogs!"

Other men took up the cry, and, eventually, some sort of order was obtained. But not for long. Suddenly the whole back and northern wings of the hotel came down with a deafening crash, as another violent shock came sweeping up from the depths of the sea-shelf on which Yokohama stands. The air was filled with smoke and dust and flying debris, while the terrified screams broke out afresh, many of them filled with the agony of those who were lying pinned beneath the ruins.

From that moment it was every man for himself. It was impossible to see through the clouds of dust and smoke, and, although the two men by the door made a gallant effort to bring out some of

2

those who remained, they could do little but reach out on chance, and, as soon as they gripped an arm, propel the owner towards where they both knew the street to be.

It says a good deal for their efforts that the casualties at the Grand were so few, but, as the big-bearded man staggered away choking, realising that he must reach the outer air or he would be overcome, he felt a further crash, and, as his companion suddenly disappeared, he knew that the gallant fellow had been caught in the full.

Despite the flames which were now roaring on every side, he tried to find him, but all to no avail; and at last he found himself out on the bund, choking and nearly suffocated, and scarcely able to see.

He lurched across to what was left of the bund wall, and, when his vision had cleared, stood gazing back at the appalling scene of destruction which was then just beginning to be revealed in all its awful magnitude.

Whichever way he looked, he saw nothing but smoke and ruins. The bund and the paved road were twisted and torn open as if some giant monster of the underworld had heaved himself bodily through the rocky crust of the globe. Farther along he could see the docks and business quarter already covered by a heavy pall of smoke, and the ships at anchor were going through grotesque acrobatics which puzzled him, until he suddenly saw one ship at one of the docks lifted bodily and carried clean across to be thrown crashing to the rocks.

A tidal wave!

As he realised that this final terror was upon the stricken place he sprang from the edge of the bund and made for the single wing of the hotel which was still standing. It was in partial ruins, and the flames would soon reach it; but he was an athletic man, and, by dint of almost superhuman effort, managed to reach a place of safely before the wave swept along its devastating course.

Crouching there, he watched, panting and cursing softly to relieve his feelings, as bodies and debris, inextricably entangled, went sweeping past him. Behind him the flames still roared, and from every side came ghastly screams of pain from some poor victim still pinned beneath the ruins and threatened by either flame or flood.

Now and then a body, detached from the debris, would float close to him; but when he saw that it contained no life he would push it gently away. Time and again this happened, until one floated in close, which he recognised by its garments as that of an European.

In this case he tried to pull the body in to the ledge beside him, and, as it turned over like a log, he gave a slight start, for all the precariousness of his position, as he saw that the features were those of a man he had known by sight and reputation—a Russian who had been knocking about Yokohama and Tokio for some weeks, and about whom he had heard several mysterious whispers.

The man was dead, and, when he had dragged him on to the ledge on which he crouched, the bearded man caught sight of the end of a thick green portfolio as the coat fell open. In a flash he had whipped it out and stuffed it into his own pocket—and in that time of stress and destruction no watching eyes perceived him do so.

As the water fell back he clambered down from his perch, and eased the dead man after him.

He laid him out of the way of the flames, and, after another look round drew out the rest of the contents of his pocket, which he stowed in his own.

Police Office fire after the earthquake /drf

EVERY newspaper and journal in every country in the world dealt in more or less detail with the appalling desolation, suffering and misery which followed on the heels of the monstrous tragedy which struck Japan.

It came without warning at the end of a hot, dry season, when every inflammable thing in the land was as dry as tinder, and roared aloft in terrible waves of flame as the devastating fire tore its way through cities and villages and hamlets.

They told, too, of the sinister typhoon that came hurtling across the yellow waters; they described the vicious onslaught of the gigantic tidal wave that swept the coast; they gave true and imaginative details which could not be exaggerated of the wailing helplessness of the stricken people who clustered together, dazed by the awfulness of this ghastly visitation which had come upon them.

On the killing, the looting, the raping and outrage by the Koreans and the escaped convicts, there is no need to dwell. It was the same as it had been in other great disasters. And, as in previous cases, heroism was discovered in the most unexpected places. The patient and the humble revealed hidden qualities of leadership, while many of those who had strutted beneath the cap of authority betrayed themselves as craven cowards, seeking only their own safety.

There was, there could be, no distinction of class during the first terrific impact of the fourfold onslaught of earthquake, typhoon, tidal wave, and fire. Every human soul within that zone of terror was but as a chip upon the sea of devastation. Colour, creed, rank— all disappeared while each fought through the sweeping horror for the life of his loved ones and himself.

And such it was, too, with the bearded, drenched, and smoke-begrimed man who clung to his precarious perch in a niche of the wreckage of the Grand Hotel on the bund of Yokohama, while the greedy water sucked and swirled about him and slowly receded with the litter of debris and human victims it had collected in its mad course.

As soon as he made sure that the water had reached its highest point and was beginning to recede, Huxton Rymer lifted his eyes and gazed out across the harbour where the tidal wave had created havoc among the craft moored at the buoys and the piers. Even at that distance he could see that the effect had been terrific, and that some of the ships and smaller boats had been literally hurled to destruction on the rocky shore.

But Rymer's gaze was for only one of those craft, and as he saw the big Messageries liner, Andre Lebon, still riding at her buoy, and apparently not seriously damaged, he drew a breath of relief.

"She has escaped." he muttered. "Will probably be held up in order to take on as many refugees as possible. But she will be one of the first out of Yokohama, and when she goes I go with her, unless—"

He did not finish the remark, but his thoughts were on the thick green leather portfolio which he had taken from the pocket of the dead man whose body the tidal wave had thrown up so close to him.

"No time to examine that now," he went on to himself. "Might be something worth while in it, or nothing at all. But it will have to wait. The first thing is to get out of here and away from Japan. There won't be any pickings of any value here for some time to come."

Once more he looked down and gave a grunt of satisfaction as he saw that the water was receding very rapidly. Already there was a good six feet between his perch and the churning surface, and if it kept up at that rate he figured he might be able to reach the ground in another half-hour. He twisted his head to right and left, looking each way along the bund, then once more he gazed out at the ships which had survived the impact of the water, and saw that, as he had opined, as many boats as possible were putting off for the shore to the succour of the pitiful groups of half-crazed natives, who were either dumb or hysterical after the ordeal through which they had just passed.

He felt mechanically for his marine glasses, forgetting for the moment that he had lost them during the uproar in the hotel. Then, as he realised they were gone, he drew out his cigarette-case and gold matchbox and found, to his relief, that he would be able to smoke.

As soon as the weed was alight he felt inside the hollow of his left arm and drew out a small automatic pistol. This he examined minutely, and in order to make sure that the cartridges were all right, pulled the trigger once. There was a sharp report as the bullet plomped into the water beneath, and Rymer gave another grunt of satisfaction as he thrust it back into its holster.

"Never can tell when I might have to use that before I get out of this hell," he muttered. "Unless I miss my guess, all Hades will break loose here as soon as night falls. I'll shoot first, and ask questions after. I am not going to take any chances of running into what I struck in Kingston after the earthquake there."

Settling himself once more, he watched the small boats as they approached the shore, and muttered something to himself as he saw them come to a stop a short distance off. This told him that those in command were taking no chances of being swamped by a mad rush on the part of the refugees; and the wisdom of the manoeuvre was soon apparent, for as soon as they had sighted the prospect of escape, thousands of persons had crowded to the very edge of the water, and some had even waded out breast high in the hope of being among the first to be succoured

Rymer watched and smoked until there was scarcely six inches of water covering the bund. Then he tossed away his cigarette, and, grasping the edge of the ledge, made his way down. As he landed in the ooze and went sloshing along the road past the ruins of the hotel, he suddenly caught sight of a band of about seven persons coming towards him. As they drew nearer he recognised them for Koreans, and his brow grew lowering as he slipped his hand inside his coat and made sure that his automatic was ready for quick action if necessary.

It was plain that the ruffians had spotted the European, too, for they quickened their pace, and Rymer knew he was in for trouble when he saw them bring up their staves and flourish their knives. Then he saw one of them point to the right, just where the northern wing of the hotel had collapsed, and as the rest of the band saw the object at which he was pointing, they seemed to lose their interest in Rymer, for they turned, and with wild shouts began running to the right.

Somewhat puzzled, Rymer kept on, and as he got past the corner of the debris he saw what it was that had attracted the ruffians. Half buried in the debris some distance above the ground, and apparently just clear of the high mark of the tidal wave, was a European, the upper part of his body free, but the lower limbs helpless beneath the load of bricks and rubble which had fallen on him.

He was quite conscious, and evidently had no misapprehensions about the menace of that oncoming band, for with great difficulty he had managed to get together a small pile of broken bricks, and was already bombarding the Koreans as they drew within distance. Rymer shot his hand inside his coat and drew out his automatic.

"Curse those yellow devils!" he snarled. "That's just about their size to cut down a man who is practically helpless and pick him clean. But they won't get away with it this time."

With that he started to run. The man whose courage, had roused Rymer's respect; saw him at that moment, and called out something in French. Rymer replied in the same language, and the next moment his pistol barked as he took a pot shot at the nearest of the ruffians.

He caught the fellow in the shoulder and sent him spinning. He coolly picked off another, and still another, and as the others saw their comrades go down they paused in their attack on the helpless Frenchman and made for Rymer.

Rymer laughed aloud as he reversed his automatic to use it as a club. He did not stand waiting for them, but rushed to meet them, and at the first impact his weapon sent one down unconscious, while his big left crashed full to the chin of another. One of the remainder managed to "get" Rymer on one shoulder with his thick bamboo stave, but before he could strike a second time Rymer had driven the blunt butt of the automatic crashing between his eyes.

The remaining Korean turned and fled, and Rymer let him go. Then, stepping over the huddled bodies of the ruffian, he sprang forward to assist the Frenchman from his precarious position.

"Take it easy, monsieur." he said. "I think we have nothing further to fear from that bunch."

The other smiled faintly.

"You did rapid and effective, work, monsieur," he said. "But I fear you will have to leave me as I am. I think one, if not both, of my legs are broken."

"Then you must be got out with no further delay," was Rymer's reply. "I am a surgeon, monsieur, so I shall move you with the least possible discomfort. Just lie as you are until I get this debris cleared away, and then I can manage a preliminary examination."

The other nodded his thanks, and Rymer set to work. He worked quickly, but with an instinctive care for the injured man, and at the end of half an hour managed to get most of the debris removed. With infinite gentleness, surprising in one of his bulk, he worked the man clear and eased him down to the ground.

Then he set to and found that the other had not been mistaken. The right femur was fractured just below the joint, while the left kneecap seemed to have suffered considerable damage, although at the moment Rymer could not tell if it was a fracture or only a dislocation.

"Do you live in Yokohama?" asked Rymer, when he had finished his examination.

"No, monsieur. I live in Paris. I have been making a tour of the East, and I came down from Tokio this morning in order to catch the Andre Lebon for Hong Kong."

"Ah! I am sailing by the same ship. I shall have to get you out to her somehow. It will be hopeless to try and get any stretcher-bearers now. Do you think you could stand it if I carried you down to the edge of the water? Some rescue boats are already at work there, and I saw several put out from the Andre Lebon. "

"But, monsieur, that would be an imposition on you, and might cause you to lose your own chance of getting away."

"Don't worry about that," answered Rymer. "I think the best means of carrying you will be pick-a-back. If you can manage to hang on to me, I can keep both hands free for use if necessary."

The wounded man saw that Rymer was determined, so he suffered himself to be picked up by his powerful rescuer, and swung round, pick-a-back fashion. Clinging on in this way, they started, Rymer picking the shortest route to the beach.

The crowds seeking succour were growing more dense each moment, and by the time Rymer reached the outskirts of the mob, he saw that he was going to have his work cut out to get himself and his burden through. Had be been alone, it would have given him little trouble but, with the necessity to pick each single step with the utmost care for the sake of the wounded man, the handicap was a serious one.

Not that the Frenchman was not being game. On the contrary, he must have been in agony every moment of the journey, but not a single groan had escaped his lips. He was clinging with his arms round Rymer's neck, his legs dangling helplessly, and the fractured thigh bone must have been giving him excruciating pain. But beyond his ashy countenance and his tightly-compressed lips from which a thin trickle of blood was oozing, he revealed no sign of what he was enduring.

At first, even in the midst of their panic, those on the fringe of the crowd instinctively gave way at the command of the big bearded European, but as he got deeper into the press, he could make scarcely any impression on that human wall, and he realised that he would have to use force.

"It is going to be tough for a bit, monsieur," he said over his shoulder. "But it is our only chance, of getting through."

"Do as you think best, my friend," responded the Frenchman. "I shall be as little hindrance to you as possible."

"Game bird!" muttered Rymer.

Then his left hand shot out and gripped the shirt of a Jap in front of him. With a single heave which scarcely brought a muscle of his torso into play, he landed the astonished Jap a good five feet away, and coolly stepped into his place. The next move was to the right, but this time the crowd immediately surrounding him had become aware of the bold efforts of the European, and there were some mutterings among them.

Rymer paid as much attention to them as he would have paid to the buzzing of so many mosquitos. He clenched his great fists, those powerful weapons that had carried him through many a tight place despite the slim, nervous fingers which marked him for the brilliant surgeon he was, and began laying about him in husky fashion.

By sheer brute force he drove on and on through the mob until he got within a few yards of the beach and within hailing distance of one of the rescue boats from the Andre Lebon. There he became stuck, and, although he sent down man after man, there was a score for each to spring up in his path, and he saw that to force that last bit of the way would cause more suffering to his burden than he could stand.

So, pausing and sweeping his arms back and forth to keep a clear space about him, he sent out a hail to the officer in the stern of the nearest rescue boat. The officer gazed about him until he saw Rymer, and lifted his hand in acknowledgment.

"Can you take us out?" bellowed Rymer through his cupped hands. "We are both travelling by the Andre Lebon."

The officer looked perplexed for a moment, then Rymer saw him give a command to his crew. Immediately the boat backed away from the shore until it was out of reach of even the most desperate of the crowd. Then he held up his hand, and when a comparative silence had fallen, he called in Japanese:

"Not another soul comes aboard this boat until you give passage to that European there." And he pointed towards Rymer.

A hundred heads were turned in the direction in which he was pointing, and as they caught sight of the scowling features of the bearded European, and then turned their eyes back to the relentless jaw of the officer, they slowly and unwillingly drew a little to one side.

Rymer wasted no time, for he knew their mood might change at any moment. Any mob is difficult enough to control, but the psychology of a mob that is driven by fear is the most baffling thing in the world.

With a cheery word to the wounded man, Rymer ploughed his way through the narrow lane of humans until he reached the edge of the water. He plunged into it and waded out waist-deep, while the boat's crew rowed in slowly. As soon as he had established contact, Rymer lifted a hand to the officer in charge of the boat, and said:

"My companion is wounded—an injured knee and a broken femur. He is a countryman of yours, and must be got aboard for treatment as quickly as possible."

In speaking, he had swung round a little, and as the officer caught sight of the wounded man's features, he gave a sharp exclamation.

"Monsieur Felibert!" he cried. "The captain told me you would be coming down from Tokio to-day, and to keep a special look-out for you. I am glad you have been rescued." Then to Rymer: "Try to get him along here, monsieur— we can ease him aboard better."

Rymer did as requested, but his movements were entirely automatic, for from the moment he had heard the officer speak the name of the wounded man, his mind had been busy and he was thinking:

"Felibert—Felibert. I remember that the papers have given considerable space to the movements of a Jules Felibert, who has been touring the East. The one referred to was stated to be a millionaire several times over, and to be a director in several big foreign development companies. I wonder if this can be the same?

"If it is—well, he ought to be a little grateful to me for rescuing him, and I shall jolly well see that he is still more indebted to me, for I shall myself do the operation on him. I guess I can fix that up with the ship's surgeon when I explain who I am, and he will certainly be glad of any assistance offered with the ship full of wounded refugees."

And it was with one of his deep grunts of satisfaction that he allowed himself to be hauled over the side of the boat.[1]

---

[1] **AUTHOR'S NOTE.**—*The good ship, Andre Lebon, named after the French admiral, Andre Lebon, is one of the fastest and most*

Several boatloads of refugees had already been transferred from the shore to the ship, and on reaching the deck Rymer found everything in a state of confusion.

His first duty was to get hold of a deck steward and find out which cabin had been allotted to M. Felibert, after which he got hold of two more stewards, and, despite the cries from every side, persuaded them to assist him to carry the wounded Frenchman down. He made him as comfortable as possible, then, after giving him a stiff brandy-and-soda to brace him up, he hurried up on deck to find the ship's doctor.

That harassed officer was in the midst of the worst cases, doing half a dozen men's work; and when Rymer spoke first, he replied curtly that he had no time to waste then. But when Rymer pressed his words home, and when the doctor finally understood that Rymer was a member of his own profession, his manner changed radically.

Rymer then explained that M. Felibert was lying in his cabin with a broken thighbone and an injured kneecap, after which he asked for permission to perform the operation, and thus relieve the ship's physician of the job. The other accepted the offer only too gladly, and when Rymer went on to say that as soon as he had finished the immediate case in hand he would return to the deck and assist there, a look of grateful relief appeared in the other's eyes.

Dr. Mineur, the ship's physician, detailed one of his orderlies to assist Rymer, and instructed the latter to conduct Rymer to the ship's surgery, where he could find all he needed for the operation. Once actively engaged in the duties of his old profession, Rymer became a

---

sumptuously fitted of the fleet operated by the Messageries Maritimes. The author travelled a portion of the coast of French Indo-Chine in this ship, and knows it well. It was actually in the port of Yokohama at the time of the recent terrible earthquake there, and reached Marseilles only some three weeks before this story was begun. The officers of the ship were brought on to Paris by the company, and were tendered a banquet in recognition of the magnificent rescue work they did at that time. The author took the opportunity to get into touch with the second in command, and the material in this story, touching on the occurrences at Yokohama following the 'quake, is as direct from the source as could be with the exception of that of an actual eye-witness.

different man. There was no thought in his mind then of criminal adventure or plotting or scheming. Before him was a case which engaged his whole attention, and particularly so for the reason that the bones of the hip and thigh had been his speciality when he had been chief surgeon at the Franz Josef Hospital in Vienna.

He finally decided to perform the operation in the surgery, so the Frenchman was brought up from his cabin and laid on the folding operating table there.

He wasted no time in getting to work. First he had a most careful and detailed examination of each injury, and nodded his head with satisfaction as he found that the knee injury was a simple crack. The other was a clean break, which he knew he could get back into place without much difficulty. His orderly acted as anaesthetist, and as soon as the patient was under the influence of the chloroform, Rymer set to work.

At any time it was a privilege to watch the master surgeon at work. Even Sexton Blake conceded that. And this occasion was no exception. As he proceeded coolly, steadily, with his long, slender, but powerful hands flashing rapidly this way, then that, the orderly stood spellbound in admiration.

That orderly had seen a good many operations in his time, but he knew that he had never watched a master such as the one before him. Deftly Rymer brought the bones into place, and swiftly applied the splints and bandages.

Then he turned his attention to the knee, which, while less severe, was quite capable of taking much longer to heal than the clean break. He applied his fingers, only using the gentle massage and coaxing of the bone that had made his name famous as a bone wizard. Then he bound it firmly, so that for some time to come the patient would be unable to move it.

As he straightened up with a sigh of relief, he turned to the orderly and gave a curt command that some stewards be fetched to take the patient back to his cabin. The man obeyed with an alacrity that he had not shown before watching the operation, and as soon as Rymer had seen his case comfortably settled he left the orderly to stand by until he should come out of the anaesthetic.

He intended returning to the deck, as he had promised, but first he went along for a whisky-and-soda, after which he repaired to his own cabin. He took care to lock the door after him; then he walked across to the porthole and drew out the green portfolio which he had found under such strange circumstances.

He opened it and peered into the different compartments. There were three in all, and in each was a thick blue envelope, sealed with heavy wax seals, but bearing no superscription. Rymer had not the slightest compunction in opening all three, and, seating himself on the side of the bunk, he began to examine them.

As he read page after page and laid it carefully aside, his cold grey eyes began to glitter like twin points of steel, and in his brain was a perfect welter of excited thought. For as he proceeded he knew that from the pocket of the dead man who had floated past him as he crouched in that niche at the Grand Hotel he had taken something that contained the greatest opportunity that had ever come his way—if he could pull it off.

When he had finished he replaced the papers in the portfolio and locked the wallet away in his steel despatch-box. Then he lit a cigarette and stood in the centre of the cabin, musing.

"It means millions—millions!" he muttered. "It's the biggest chance I have ever been up against, and I must—I will—pull it off. But it is going to take more money than I can lay hands on now to finance it, and there is no time to waste.

"It may be thought that the portfolio has been lost with the man who was carrying it, but sooner or later the people who are behind this deal will get wise to the fact that it is still in existence.

"But no matter. It is like a bearer cheque—the man who holds it is the bird who will collect the money. And Huxton Rymer is the one who is going to do the collecting. Millions! There might be a chance of getting something out of this man Felibert, if he is the one I think he is. Anyway, Rymer, my boy, your care is to cultivate him as much as possible on the way to Hong Kong, and gently keep his gratitude uppermost."

With that he tossed the end of his cigarette through the open port, and went upon deck to assist Dr. Mineur. And as the big-bearded adventurer moved about, working quickly and efficiently, it is a safe bet that not a single soul dreamed for a moment that the mind behind those forceful grey eyes was almost entirely engaged with the startling stroke he had made, and that his bodily movements were almost entirely mechanical.

But then they did not know Huxton Rymer!

When Rymer had dragged the man on to the ledge on which he crouched, he caught sight of the end of a thick green portfolio as the coat fell open. In a flash he had whipped it out and stuffed it into his own pocket—and in that time of stress and destruction no watching eyes perceived him do so. *(Chapter 1.)*

"Can you take us out?" bellowed Rymer, with the injured Frenchman dangling helplessly from his shoulders. The officer on the boat held up his hand. "Not another soul comes aboard this boat till you give passage to that European there!" he shouted to the panic-stricken crowd. (*Chapter 2.*)

SOME four months after the disastrous earthquake in Japan Mr. Blake, the well-known London criminologist, was seated at his desk in the consulting-room, at Baker Street, listening attentively to two gentlemen who, from what he had so far been able to gather, had a case of considerable importance to lay before him.

Although both were dressed fashionably, and were undoubtedly of high social standing, they were, nevertheless, oddly assorted, for while one was typical of the well-groomed City man, the other was small of stature and of Japanese nationality.

On Blake's desk lay their cards. The Englishman's was inscribed as follows:

| **Mr. ALGERNON BIRKMIRE.** |
| **Voyagers' Club, Pall Mall.** |

And the Japanese gentleman's ran thus:

| **Baron TAYASHI,** |
| **Tokio, Japan.** |
| |
| **Diplomatic Club,** |
| **London.** |

The whole City of London knew Mr. Algernon Birkmire as a rich and influential financier, head of the well-known firm of Birkmire & Co. And as for Baron Tayashi, he was almost as well known in London as in his native city of Tokio, where he was a director in half a dozen banks, silk houses, and cotton firms, and whose name was one to conjure with in the whole Far East.

It had been Mr. Birkmire who had taken upon himself the burden of explaining to Blake the details of the problem which they had come to lay before him. After a few preliminary remarks dealing with the subject in general, he had settled down to give Blake full details, and Blake was sitting with steady, thoughtful eyes behind the intermittent clouds of blue that rose from his Havana, giving his whole attention to what his visitor was saying.

"The whole business, is rather complicated, Mr. Blake," said the financier, after a brief pause, during which he glanced at his companion. "To explain just what I mean, it will be necessary for me to go back a few years. In fact, back to the time of the Russo-Japanese War about twenty years ago. At that time, as you know, the Japanese succeeded in getting control of most of Korea, which, up to then, had been dominated by the Russians.

"Of course, the natural sequence of events followed. All, or most of the various Russian concessions were cancelled by the Japs, and a lot of new country thrown open to their own people and friendly foreigners for development. I may say, in passing, that one of the companies, in which both Baron Tayashi and myself are interested, succeeded in getting several quite valuable concessions, thanks to my friend's influence with his own government.

"But that is apart from the present case. Just before the Russo-Japanese War broke out the late Count Witte had signed what was probably the greatest concession in Korea. It covered something like a hundred thousand square miles in area, and, apart from its valuable timber, possessed and does possess almost unlimited quantities of rich minerals, coal, and oil.

"One of the first things the Japanese tried to do, once they got control of Korea, was to annul that concession. There was some difficulty in doing so as certain powerful German interests were involved, and they naturally put up a strenuous fight to retain it.

"In the meantime my friend, Baron Tayashi, was corresponding with me, and suggested that, owing to the friendship existing between our two countries, and our personal business connections, we should make an attempt to have the concession made over to us, he to use his influence out there, while I was to arrange financial matters at this end.

"The struggle in the courts was still going on when the last War broke out, and of necessity everything was held up. But not long after the signing of peace we restarted negotiations, and just about six months ago managed to get the former concession annulled. That did not mean that it was transferred to us. Instead of following some such course, the Japanese Government—wisely, as I think—called for tenders for the whole of the concession, stipulating that one quarter of all nett profits should go to their Korean administration.

"We followed the affair very closely, and on the advice of my friend, Baron Tayashi, I interested my friends here in London, and we tendered. I do not know, of course, whether ours was the highest tender or not. But, in any event, the Japanese Government accepted our tender, and gave us an open concession to the whole thing.

"Now, here is where the crux of the whole matter comes in. At the time of tendering, the tender was sent in under the joint names of Barron Tayashi and myself on behalf of a syndicate to be formed in case we were successful. As I have already said, we were, and I was engaged in forming the syndicate here when the terrible earthquake occurred.

"On the very day of that disaster Baron Tayashi's partner in Tokio was to send along the actual concession. It had been left open, so to say, for the name of the syndicate here to be inserted, as, when the papers were drawn, I had not registered the syndicate under any official name.

"As soon as the cables were in working order we discovered that the special messenger—a Russian—left Tokio, intending to catch one of the Messageries steamers for Marseilles. It was difficult to discover much more.

"Baron Tayashi's own block of business buildings in Tokio, where nearly all of his interests were concentrated, were completely destroyed by the earthquake and fire. Some of his papers, which were in a fire-proof safe, were recovered intact, but, owing to the appalling suddenness with which the earthquake struck, there was no time to save any of the books and papers which were in use during the day's business.

"To make matters worse, Baron Tayashi's partner, several of his executives, and a large number of the personnel were killed or burned to death. For weeks he endeavoured to find out something about the actual condition of affairs. He left London and made personal investigations in Tokio and Yokohama. What results he obtained about his numerous private interests is apart from this matter.

"It is sufficient to say that he ascertained for an absolute fact that the special messenger had actually left Tokio before the earthquake, and must have been in Yokohama or very near that city when the upheaval took place. We know this because his body was recovered some days after the disaster on the beach about two miles west of Yokohama. But although Baron Tayashi followed up every possible channel of inquiry, he was unable to find a single trace of the papers which had been entrusted to the care of the unfortunate messenger.

"Shortly after Baron Tayashi returned to London. As you know, the whole of the attention of the government was, and still is, given primarily to alleviating the sufferings of the thousands who were ruined by the disaster. It was useless to attempt to bring up the question of the Korean concession then, and my friend thought the wiser course was to wait until a more favourable opportunity. He advised this on his return, and I agreed with him.

"At that we left it, although, of course, we had a man in Tokio ready to approach the government for a new concession as soon as their domestic problems should be straightened out. That was roughly a month ago.

"Since then we have discovered quite a few things. Firstly, it would appear that while the messenger carrying the documents perished, the portfolio in which he carried the letter fell into the hands of other persons.

"We know this because Baron Tayashi's secret agents in the Far East have advised him that a foreign group has appeared in Korea and has taken over the whole concession which was ours by right. Even if the Japanese Government could give its attention to the matter at present, it would at the best mean a repetition of what went before just long weary months of legal delays, and, of course, new tenders being called for if we won.

"Baron Tayashi has canvassed all the possibilities by cable, and he has been advised by his political friends in Japan that the only chance of handling the matter quickly is to take direct action. By that I mean to go straight to the spot and try to do something there.

"Of course, you know, Mr. Blake, that Korea is full of intrigue. The Bolshevists and the Chinese are bitterly opposing the Japanese there, and the Koreans themselves dislike being under the Japs. In those circumstances you can see that scores of chances would arise and would be seized in order to keep us out.

"If the documents had not been left open for the insertion of the name of the syndicate it would have been more simple, as those who have jumped our claim, so to say, would have been forced to commit forgery. But they have probably used bribery on a big scale, and no doubt have come to some secret arrangement whereby the Koreans, the Chinese, and the Bolshevists benefit, as well as offering to the Japanese Government the quarter share stipulated in the concession.

"In the present confused state of affairs in Japan it would take months, and possibly years, to cut through all the red tape and oust them from the ground by ordinary legal means. And I don't mind confiding to you that the concession is quite rich enough to stand all those calls on it and still pay a very handsome profit to the company that develops it.

"That is the problem, Mr. Blake, which Baron Tayashi and I have come to lay before you. Can you help us in the direct action I mentioned?"

Blake relaxed his position and carefully flicked the ash from his cigar before answering. Then:

"That all depends on how far you are prepared to go," he said thoughtfully, "I gather that these persons into whose hands the concession has fallen are already doing some preliminary work on the ground?"

"They are. Baron Tayashi's secret agents have cabled him that a large party has arrived, and that no fewer than six engineers are employed in the preliminary survey to find out just what the prospects are. I should have mentioned that, from what we have been told, we suspect the parties who have jumped the claim are connected with the same German interests who had the concession before the War. Over a hundred Europeans in all are now there, and several hundred coolies have been taken on. Further than that we do not know what progress they have made."

"Um! They appear to have lost no time! Well, let us just look at one or two items you have mentioned.

"From what you have said, it would seem that in some way the portfolio containing the documents relating to the concession fell into the hands of outsiders either before or after the messenger died. From what I have read of the confusion that followed in both Yokohama and Tokio, there would only be about one chance in a hundred thousand or so that any person finding the portfolio by accident would realise its value. Certainly, no ordinary Japanese would do so.

"We might assume that it was found by a European, who, on reading the contents, knew how valuable the papers were. Alternatively, we must allow for the chance that it was known to persons interested that the concession was coming through to London by special messenger, and in that case the man was probably shadowed for some time, and followed as soon as he left Baron Tayashi's building in Tokio.

"The fact that you suspect the same German interests who

worked the concession before the War, or, at least, were preparing to develop it, seems to lend colour to that theory. But that can rest for the present.

"We can take it for granted that the blanks have been filled in by the present holders of the documents, and, since there has undoubtedly been a good deal of crooked work on their part, they know that their claim only holds while the papers are in their possession. In other words, if they lost the documents a new application to the Japanese Government would possibly enable Baron Tayashi to secure once more the same concession. Am I correct?"

"Perfectly!" answered the Englishman and the Jap in one voice.

"You speak of 'direct action,' " pursued Blake. "To me it seems that direct action would mean nothing more or less than the stealing of those documents. Rather a strong term to use, but that is what it means. Am I to understand that you wish me to arrange the matter in that way?"

"I suppose that is what it really amounts to," remarked the financier. "Of course, I am not suggesting that you should do anything contrary to the laws of this country or any other, Mr. Blake. But— well, you see just the position we are in."

Blake smiled.

"Have you any idea as to the whereabouts of the documents?"

"We have talked that over and have agreed that the most likely place is in Korea."

"That would seem the most reasonable assumption. Then what you really wish is for me either to go out to Korea and get possession of those papers, or send someone else to do so?"

"I don't see any other way in which we can outwit them."

Blake smiled thoughtfully for the space of perhaps a couple of minutes; then his eyes opened wide, and he looked first at the financier, then at the baron.

"All right, gentlemen," he said crisply, "I'll take on the case. Let us get down to business. I want to be in possession of every item that may help me."

An expression of relief came into the eyes of his two visitors, and they drew their chairs nearer, while Tinker, who had been seated at his desk in the corner, listening closely to what was being said, got up and brought across his notebook to jot down the data as it was given to Blake.

The Fourth Chapter. The Peril of the Yellow Sea.

ON a clear sunny day in early spring a big Chinese junk was beating its way close inshore where the China coast lay drear and desolate in rocky humps, which looked like so many gigantic camels resting at the edge of the Yellow Sea after completing some fabulous caravan journey.

At times the grotesque-looking sail of another junk could be seen, and, occasionally the smoke of a freighter coming down from Port Arthur, but for the greater part the big junk was alone in the solitude of the sea which washed that desolate shore.

It was not a North China junk, that, nor did it possess the ordinary matting sail of the Canton junks. In place of the matting was canvas, and aboard there was an unusual air of neatness and general ship-shapeness which is decidedly foreign to the craft of China.

Nevertheless, it had come from very close to Canton, for, two weeks before, it had slipped out of Kowloon, on the main coast opposite Hong Kong, and ever since had been wallowing along up the coast inside the island of Formosa, thence past Shanghai, and on into the Yellow Sea.

It had hugged the China coast closely the whole way, although it did not attempt to put in at any port until it reached Tsi-nan close to Kiao-Chow. Even there, it had lain at anchor for only half a day, while some necessary supplies were brought aboard; then it had started again, and from that point began making a course which would bring it away from the China mainland just before reaching Wei-hai-wai, the recent British spot on the Yellow Sea which lies just across from Seul in Korea.

On the day in question it was creeping along towards a rocky point, where it was the intention to change the course and begin the run across the narrow waist of the Yellow Sea to Seul. By calculation, that point should be reached in the early evening, thus permitting the crossing to be made during the dark hours of the night.

From the care with which the big junk had avoided touching at any of the larger ports, it can be guessed that those on board had certain reasons for their movements being unheralded up and down the coast. As a matter of fact, that was exactly the case, and there were two persons in the ship's company whose intention it was, if possible, to slip into Seul without passing through the usual formalities.

There was little to distinguish the pair from the rest of those on board. They were both dressed in the ordinary garb of Chinese coolies, although they took no part in the work of the junk other than what they chose to do for the sake of daily exercise. And yet, those two were treated with profound respect by the head serang of the junk, and by all the members of the crew as well.

The subtle complexes of the Chinese mind has been a byword for centuries, and there exist very few persons among the "foreign devils" who have ever succeeded in penetrating behind the yellow veil of bland negation which the Celestial uses as a mask.

One of the very few is that strange and mysterious man known among the Chinese themselves as the veritable-and-much-to-be-respected Hsui-Fsi, some time the real power behind the Manchu throne, but of late years living in the House of the Silver Moon in the heart of San Francisco's Chinatown.

And there were possibly not more than half a dozen living persons who knew that Hsui-Fsi was, in reality, an English gentleman, none other than Sir Gordon Saddler, who had been one of the wildest of the young bucks about London in the late fifties and early sixties of last century.

Another was the famous London criminologist, Mr. Sexton Blake, of Baker Street, who had more than once passed through the most dangerous haunts to be found in the teeming cities of the great country of the Yellow Dragon, with never the quiver of a suspicion that he was not exactly what he appeared to be.

In passing, it is worthy of note that Sexton Blake and the "Mystery Man of 'Frisco " were on the most friendly and confidential terms, had combined forces more than once to root out certain phases of intrigue in China, and that Sexton Blake was one of the half-dozen or so persons who knew the real identity of Hsui-Fsi.

Therefore, when the inborn secretiveness of the Chinese nature is taken into account, it is not difficult to understand how it was that the big junk could beat her way up from Kowloon and on into the Yellow Sea with never a whisper of her real purpose leaking out. On top of that, a very handsome charter fee to the chief serang, and a substantial bonus to each member of the crew, had effectually sealed any possibility of betrayal, for from the chief serang down to the youngest deck-boy, it was known what would be their fate at the hands of a certain very powerful Chinese gentleman in Hong Kong if a single rumour got abroad.

The serang's instructions had been to enter the port of Seul in Korea as unobtrusively as possible, and to lend every aid to the two coolies who had come aboard at Kowloon to get into the town without any suspicion being roused as to their real identity.

He had faithfully followed those instructions, and on that warm spring afternoon it looked as if the next morning would see his mission accomplished. It was along towards early evening that the course of the junk was changed, so that by dusk she would be well off the rocky headland that could be just glimpsed in the distance, and by the time full night had fallen would be running before a strong breeze across the narrow waist of the Yellow Sea for her objective.

As the huge, quaintly-shaped sail flattened out, the two coolies who had been standing at the side watching the manoeuvre, turned away and made their way aft to the odd, high-pitched poop which completely dominated the stern. Standing by the gigantic tiller, where he could keep a sharp eye on the dozen or so men away forward who were working at the ponderous sweeps, was the serang, and, as the two coolies paused close to the low entrance through which one could descend by a bamboo ladder to the roughly-beamed saloon below, he made a remark in Cantonese to the taller of the pair. The latter nodded and gazed for a few seconds back towards the dreary coast which they had been hugging all day.

"If the wind holds you will have succeeded," he said. "It is fair now, but look!" And he pointed astern to where the eastern sky was banked with a heavy purple cloud. "If that overtakes us," he continued, "we may be driven from our course."

The serang followed the direction of his gaze.

"We shall beat it, master" (strange expression to use to a coolie) he said confidently. "The Yellow Sea is treacherous at this time of the year, but I have sailed these waters before, and I know its moods."

The tall coolie nodded, and, without another word, descended, followed by his shorter and younger companion. As they dropped to the floor of the saloon a Chinese boy appeared as if by magic, bearing a large lacquered tray on which was a pot of finest Suchong tea, wafer thin tea vases, and a pile of strange-looking sweetmeats.

He placed the tray on the table, and, with a low salaam, retired. The two coolies then seated themselves, and while the elder drew a packet of yellow cigarettes from under his shirt, the younger proceeded to pour out the tea. The other watched him for a few minutes, then the yellow countenance broke as he smiled in what was distinctly un-Chinese fashion.

"You'll do, my lad," he said, in cultured English. "When you left Kowloon I think you said nothing on earth would ever make you grow used to Suchong and sweetmeats. That was only a couple of weeks ago, Tinker, and now you are as anxious for it each evening as any Chinese lad."

The younger of the pair grinned as no Chinese lad could ever grin.

"Well, guv'nor, I'll give in to you about that. But there is something about this muck that gets hold of one. At first these darned messes made me feel sick, but they're not so bad when your stomach gets over the insult."

The elder, who, as it may have been guessed, was none other than Sexton Blake, smiled faintly as he sipped a little of the fragrant Suchong.

"I expect you will grow up one day, Tinker. Your stomach seems to consider everything an insult except some very dubious forms of—er—food which keeps me mystified. However, each to his own, I suppose, but Heaven help your stomach.

"As for the food of the Chinese, they claim with some pride that away back, while our ancestors were still naked and woad-painted cave-men, they had already evolved the true theory of eating, and I have heard many prominent specialists say that the Chinese sequence of foods is as nearly perfect in relation to the material needs of the human system as one could well devise."

"Well, if that forty-course banquet we once went to in Hong Kong with your friend the comprador is a sample of that, then excuse me," replied Tinker, with a shudder. "Gee, guv'nor, I didn't know half the time whether we were eating hundred-year-old eggs or rats-tails!"

Blake laughed, then his face resumed the immobility of the character he had assumed.

"We are nearing the end of the first stage, my lad," he said presently. "If the serang is a true prophet, then we should slip into Seul to-morrow morning. But I don't like the look of the weather in the east. If one of the sudden hurricanes for which this bit of sea is notorious should hit us in the night it will, at the very least, delay us, and we shall have to beat about and try to make an entry to-morrow night instead.

"We can't afford to take the slightest risk. From the moment we enter Seul every retreat will have been cut off except what we may be able to devise as circumstances suggest. And, as I warned you before we left Kowloon, don't for one moment forget that the moment our real identity is suspected our lives won't be worth the price of a toda of rice."

"I'll not forget that, guv'nor," promised Tinker. "I know enough now to respect the Chinkie even if I don't like some of his ways."

Blake nodded, and as they had finished their light repast, rose to go back on deck. As they emerged from the companion he once more cast his eyes astern, and, although he had resumed his outward expressionless mask, he was saying to himself that he didn't like that threatening bank of cloud hanging in the east.

During the short time they had been below, it had crept up a considerable distance, until the sharply-defined edge was almost directly over them. Above and to the west the sky was still clear, but there was a "feel" in the air that Blake knew only too well, and, despite the confidence of the serang, he would have liked it much better if they were then farther across towards Seul.

He said nothing, however, and the pair made their way along to the waist, where they stood by the side watching the progress of the junk. She was a newly-built junk, and with modern canvas on her, instead of matting, could outsail the average craft of her kind. Looking to the west and ahead, everything seemed as right and trim as could be desired. But astern there was creeping, creeping that threatening bank, and if it hit them abeam Blake knew only too well what it could, and possibly would, do to them.

They remained on deck for another couple of hours, when a "boy" came to call them to the evening repast. The sun had gone down some time since, and the western sky was bright with stars. In the east nothing could be seen but an impenetrable wall of black, at the very edge of which, and almost directly over them, shone a single brilliant cosmic sun, which was obliterated even as Blake gazed up at it.

The bank seemed to be climbing more quickly than had been the case an hour or so before.

They ate the evening meal in silence, and once more returned to the deck. There was little change to be seen there, and, since the serang seemed as confident as ever that they would beat the gathering storm, Blake decided that they should turn in, in order to be well prepared for what was to come on the morrow.

Their luggage was of the simplest. Sexton Blake was an old stager, and he knew how futile it would have been to expect to achieve the purpose which had brought him and Tinker to Korea, if either of them retained any of the usual appurtenances which a European might carry.

Therefore, before leaving Kowloon they had discarded every single item which could rouse suspicion, with the exception of certain toilet articles which it was their intention to leave on the junk, and, of course, their automatic pistols, which they carried well concealed under their loose pants.

In addition both wore money-belts under their shirts, in which they had stuffed some gold and silver pieces—and in one pocket of Blake's were certain papers which he might need as occasion arose. These papers were enclosed in a waterproof covering, for, since it was their intention to penetrate into the interior, back of Seul, it was impossible to tell what difficulties of stream and forest they might encounter.

Their bedding, too, was a compromise between the mat of the Celestial and the mattress of the Occidental, but those, of course, would be left behind on the junk. After a final cigarette they rolled under the blankets, and, while Tinker dropped off to sleep within a few minutes, Blake lay on his back, his eyes wide open and his ears ready to catch the first sound of the threatening hurricane.

Nothing came, however, but the usual sounds of the junk—the pad, pad of naked feet as one of the crew trotted along above, the swish and rush and gurgle of the water as the junk lumbered her way along before the land breeze, the creak of the blocks, and the whining of cordage as the craft dipped and wallowed in the lazy sea.

Eventually he, too, slept, and for the next three hours knew nothing of what was passing above. But at the end of that time there came a terrific crash, as something went down on deck before the first wild blast of the storm that had overtaken them.

As he sat up Blake felt the junk pause, then stagger like a wounded thing as the crazy hurricane tore into her as if it would flatten her to the face of the sea.

The spring storms, which are such a bane in the Yellow Sea, are not as severe as the summer and early autumn typhoons that spring up so suddenly on the China Coast, but a really bad one can almost be ranked as a typhoon, and the moment he heard the peculiar whine of the torrent of wind which had assailed them Sexton Blake knew that they had been hit by a real hummer.

Blake turned his head, and by the light of the small lantern which swung overhead saw that Tinker had just woke up.

"What is it?" he asked sleepily.

"The storm has struck us, and, unless I am mistaken, it is going to give us a pretty dance before it finishes with us. Better get up on deck, I think, and see how the junk is behaving. Put on that sacking cape you have."

Tinker tumbled out from beneath his blankets, and began searching for the rough burlap, covering which he had brought along from Kowloon as the sort of protective garment a coolie would have with him. Blake was similarly engaged, and as soon as they had adjusted the wraps they emerged from the cabin and climbed the bamboo ladder to the poop.

Despite his confidence, the serang had put an additional four men on to handle the great sweep-like tiller, and, even at that, they were having all they could do to keep the junk on her course as she wallowed and groaned under the terrific onslaught of the storm. Blake and the lad were forced to cling on with all their strength, and they had just managed to crawl along to a position where the side offered a little protection when the rain came.

It was appalling, smothering, completely overwhelming, and yet it served to flatten down, to some extent, the sea, which had been lashed to a crazy fury by the tearing gale of wind which had struck before the rain. Leaving Tinker clinging to a coir-rope under the lee side of the poop, Blake managed to work his way along to where the serang was lashed to the long tiller. They tried to converse, but in that pandemonium their words were clipped and flung into the night by the raging wind and rain.

Blake gave it up, and struggled back to where Tinker was waiting. By dint of getting his mouth close to the lad's ear and shouting with all the lung-power he possessed, he managed to make the lad hear the one word, "cabin," and when he turned, Tinker began creeping along after him.

Somehow they managed to make the companionway and slide down the bamboo ladder to the saloon—if such it might be called. There they could make themselves heard.

"It's going to be worse than I expected," he said. "She's a good craft, Tinker, but all the fiends and devils of the storm-god are out there to-night! It is as bad as a pukkha typhoon, and I don't like our running before it. The serang can't bring the junk round now —we would turn turtle the first second the wind got us sideways. But he should have changed his course before. I gave him plenty of warning, and he should have taken precautions. It is too late now!"

"Do you think the junk will weather it, guv'nor?"

"I can't make a guess. If it is a brief storm we stand a good chance. If it lasts for some hours, Heaven only knows where we will land up by morning! Anyway, we can't do anything on deck. Those fellows know best how to handle their own craft. Nevertheless, we shall stick here and be ready for whatever comes. If it comes to the worst, we must do our best to try and stick together."

"There are some rather primitive sort of lifebelts in the cabin," remarked Tinker. "Do you think I had better get them?"

"It might be as well!" agreed Blake.

As the lad went off, Blake took a deep gulp at his peg, then frowned moodily at the rough table.

"Couldn't have hit us at a worse time," he muttered. "I don't see how the junk can possibly weather this, but I mustn't tell the lad that, yet. We can only be prepared—that's all. But, even if we do get to land safely, it is difficult to see what complications may arise there now. If I thought we had a chance, I would go on deck and try to persuade the serang to change the course; but we haven't—not an earthly. So it's just sit tight and see what happens!"

Tinker returned just then, and the pair sat in silence, gripping the edge of the rough table for support, and wondering at each frenzied dip of the fighting junk if it would be the last or not. Two hours, three hours went by, then, as he tossed away the end of what was probably his sixth or seventh cigarette, Blake rose.

"It seems to be getting a little easier, my lad," he said. "Let us try the deck again."

Tinker started to rise, but, even as he did so, there came a devastating crash, followed by another and another, and both he and

Blake were hurled with terrific force against the bulkhead as the junk came to a dead stop and then began crashing with sickening blows as the waves tore at her and hurled her again and again upon the rocks into which she had plunged.

Together Blake and Tinker made one wild effort, and just managed to grasp the spar as it was lifted over the junk's side. They clung close together and waited what Fate might decide to do next. (*Chapter 5*)

The Fifth Chapter.   The Coolie Castaways.

THEY managed to get to their feet somehow, and made a concerted movement towards the bamboo ladder. The saloon was now at an angle of something like fifty degrees, but that was changing to a greater or lesser slope after each crash. The junk was completely helpless as her life was being battered out and, stout though her timbers were, it was only too obvious that she would begin to break up soon. No hulk ever came off the slips that could have withstood the combined onslaught of wave and wind and rock.

Blake boosted Tinker through to the deck, and, as he himself crawled after, he could see not a single sign of either the serang or the crew. It was pitch dark, but, even at that, he had heard the mast come tumbling down soon after the junk had struck. The probability was, he figured, that all hands had been swept overboard, and, later on, he discovered that this was so.

For the moment he had his hands full to look after himself and Tinker. They hadn't the remotest notion where they had struck. That the hurricane had carried the junk before it, and had played with it at will, was all they knew. It was a fairly safe guess that they had struck on the Korean coast somewhere, or on some of the jagged reefs that lie just east of Seul. But, on the other hand, since the gale had swept up from the south-east, it might well be that they had been carried past Seul and had struck beyond that port.

The immediate problem was to try and find out what chances they had— whether to cling desperately to that crashing hulk of the junk, or to cast themselves into the sea and trust to the buoyancy of their primitive lifebelts, and their own swimming powers, to enable them to scramble up on some spot where they would be out of reach of the sea.

The question was settled for them, for, as they clung on to the rope which had been strung along beside the poop, a giant wave threw something against them with terrific force.

Both were nearly flattened against the poop by the force of the impact, but as a lurch of the junk caused the object to slide away, Blake grabbed Tinker by the arm and propelled him forward. He had grasped just in time that it was a loose spar that was being carried free by the waves.

Together they made one wild effort, and just managed to grasp the spar as it was lifted over the side. They clung close together and waited for what Fate might decide to do next. For good or bad, the junk was now beyond their reach, and Heaven only knew what would happen next.

The water was not very cold. Korea lies, roughly, in about the same latitude as Gibraltar, but, whereas the latter is still subject to the cold vagaries of the Atlantic during the early months of spring, the Yellow Sea washes the lower coast of Korea, and the Shantung district of China is affected by a warm current that has its genesis somewhere down in the vicinity of the Philippines, or the Spice Islands, and in southern Korea spring comes as swiftly as it is heralded by the Chinook winds in Western Canada.

At the same time, it must be remembered that Blake and Tinker were garbed in nothing but the thin cotton clothes which the ordinary coolie wears, and what chill there was in the water soon penetrated to their blood.

They could do nothing to mitigate this. The sea was running too high, the night was as black as the pit of Tophet, and it took every atom of strength each possessed to cling to the spar, which was being tossed about like a cork.

No words could pass between them. While the force of the storm had undoubtedly abated, the wind was still shrieking too loudly for human words to bridge a distance of even three feet, so the two Britishers, in no strange position when compared with other incidents in the career of the Baker Street pair, but certainly undergoing one of the most strenuous tests that they had even been up against, just hung on and waited for the best—or the worst.

For an hour or better, they clung to their frail refuge, being tossed hither and thither without sensing the slightest sign of either rocks or shore. For the former Blake was devoutly thankful. For the latter he was puzzled, for if the junk had piled herself up on some stray rock, then their hopes of reaching the shore would be pretty well nil.

On the other hand, if they had been piled up on the main coast, then it was a pretty good chance that, sooner or later, wind and tide and waves would throw the spar up somewhere.

Once, and only once, Blake thought he was able to make out a patch which seemed a little blacker than the stormy sky, and which, he guessed, might be what was left of the junk. But before he could be sure it had disappeared, and they were swept on again at the will of the forces which had beset them.

Gradually, almost imperceptibly, the darkness seemed to grow a little thinner. There was nothing exactly to gauge this by. It was more sense of the change than anything else. But in another half-hour they both saw that it was perceptibly less dark, and they knew dawn was coming.

They clung on with slightly renewed hopes until there could be no doubt that the eastern sky was growing grey, and as a cold, wet dawn revealed the dividing line between sea and sky they gazed eagerly about them, trying to find some trace of land.

It was Tinker who saw it first. The storm had eased sufficiently now, for him to make himself heard. He shouted, and, freeing one arm, pointed over Blake's left shoulder.

Blake turned his head and saw the barren line which the lad had spotted. It was mainland. There could be no doubt of that, and he knew it was probably the Korean coast either above or below Chemulpo, which is the port for Seul, the capital.

It took another half-hour for them to discover that the spar was being slowly but surely carried shorewards, and as there was not the faintest sign of the wrecked junk, it began to look as if that one desperate hope they had grasped had been the best bet in the chaos of wind and rain and heaving sea.

It seemed an eternity of time to the haggard pair before the shore line appeared really close. By now they could see that it was of the same bleak formation as the Shantung coast which they had left the preceding afternoon. If the storm had not abated, there was not a doubt that the driving sea would have hurled the spar on to the rocks with such ruthless force that they would have both been ground to pulp.

But each moment the waves were growing more tranquil, and when at last the spar did ground, they had little difficulty in scrambling along it until they could make a safe landing.

They staggered up the barren beach, and with one accord dropped down on the rubble just above the highest spot which the sea could reach. They were exhausted mentally and physically.

Blake had no need to tell Tinker that now was no time for them to rest. Every moment's delay would be dangerous. But not even Blake knew that there was an additional danger in a small, dirty-looking tramp steamer that suddenly appeared from the east. He watched it for a moment. Then he said:

"We'll give ourselves about half an hour, my lad. Then we shall have to make a move. I have a feeling that we are somewhere north, above Chemulpo, which means that if we are to make Seul we shall have to hoof it to the east. It is deserted-looking country just here, but we may meet someone on the road of whom we can ask the way.

"As far as I can figure out. we are the only ones who escaped from the junk. Heaven knows where she is now, but I think the serang and the crew must have been swept into the sea when she first struck. I am sorry indeed if that is the case, but in a rather coldblooded way it aids us in getting into the country without being suspected."

Tinker was too fagged to speak. He simply nodded his agreement with what his master said, and, gouging out holes in the rubble for his shoulder and hip, was off to sleep in less than a minute. Blake did not lie down. He sat broodingly gazing out to sea at the rusty little tramp that was steaming up and down in a most erratic way.

"I wonder what she is about?" he asked himself. "Perhaps she has been sent out by the Chemulpo authorities to see what toll of wreckage the storm took last night. Well, if she finds the junk, I am willing to wager she will only find a battered hulk."

For a full half-hour he sat thus; then he reached over and shook the sleeping Tinker. The lad stumbled to his feet, and a moment later they made their way inland through a belt of low scrub until they came to a rough track that seemed to follow the coast line.

There Blake paused for a moment; then he turned east, and they set off at a forced pace under a warming sun, in the hope that they would pick up Chemulpo.

For a couple of hours or so they trudged along, feeling better and better under the exercise and invigorating sun that had burst through the passing storm clouds, although they were beginning to feel acutely the pangs of hunger.

It was only after that length of time that they saw in the distance the first human beings on that desolate shore— a couple of natives approaching, each of whom was supporting a long bamboo stick, at each end of which hung a basket.

As they drew together Blake halted them, and in the lingua franca of the coast asked them guardedly if he and his companion were on the right track for Chemulpo. To his relief he was told that it was but two hours' journey to the east. Next, he asked if the other pair possessed any food, and, if so, would they sell some.

There was some argument over this, but at last he managed to exchange a piece of silver for a measure of cold cooked rice and soya beans, and, with friendly gestures, the two natives passed on.

As soon as they were out of sight, Blake and Tinker dropped down by the roadside and consumed the rough fare. At one side there were innumerable little pools remaining from the torrent of rain which had swept the coast the night before, so there was no difficulty in slaking their thirst.

From under his shirt Blake drew out his waterproof case of cigarettes and waterproof matchbox, and he and Tinker had the luxury of an enjoyable smoke.

Then it was onwards again, and at the end of an hour there could be no doubt that they were approaching some large centre of human habitation, for they came upon many little groups of natives heading in each direction; some who had been at the market of the day before and had been detained in Chemulpo on account of the storm, the others just making for the market which would be held the following day.

Apart from the Koreans there were Mongolians of half a dozen different breeds—Japs, Chinese, and various crossbreeds, which could only be classified as mongrels. Therefore, in joining one of the groups there was nothing to single out Blake and Tinker apart from the rest, except Blake's physique, which was not enough to create any real suspicion.

It was just on midday when they passed through the western gate of the port. As soon as they were within the walls Blake took care to separate himself and Tinker from the group they had joined. He had a certain letter tucked inside one of the pockets of his belt, addressed to a Japanese merchant of the place, and he was anxious to get it delivered as soon as possible.

During the Russo-Japanese War Blake had been in Korea on a special mission which had taken him on to Port Arthur, and had kept him there for some days during the siege of that place. Therefore he remembered both Chemulpo and Seul fairly well, and his first objective was to make in the direction of the centre of the city, where were located the offices of the Japanese merchant to whom he bore the letter.

The building in which these offices were situated was in the centre of the business district which had been built up since the Japanese occupation, and on a square where the two modern erections had been grouped together. They reached this square without incident, and as they approached the Cho-Sen Hotel, Blake glanced at it with a whimsical thought in his mind, for it was at that modern hostelry he had stayed when last in Chemulpo,

But just as they reached it his thoughts changed abruptly, and his fingers barely brushed the sleeve of the young coolie who was shuffling along beside him.

At that moment a big bearded man had just emerged from the hotel, and was standing at the edge of the kerb in the act of lighting a cigar before entering the rickshaw which was obviously waiting for him.

The lad looked ahead and saw what Blake had meant him to see. As they passed the European their faces were as blank as the mask of any Celestial, but both of them had recognised in the big, well-dressed European none other than an old enemy—no one less, in fact, than Dr. Huxton Rymer.

（京 157）　　　HONMACHI STREET. SEOUL　　　目丁三町本城京　　　（所名鮮朝）

/drf

EVEN after they were a considerable distance past Rymer neither Blake nor Tinker made any comment on the startling incident of finding the notorious criminal-adventurer in Korea.

Nevertheless, Blake's mind was working swiftly. He would not have been greatly surprised at finding Rymer bobbing up in any part of the globe, and he knew perfectly well that the crook would not be in a place like Chemulpo unless he were after big pickings of some kind.

It was but natural, in considering all the possibilities, that Blake should weigh the chances of Rymer being mixed up with the gang that had "jumped" the concession of the Anglo-Japanese company which he was acting for. He couldn't quite figure how Rymer could have got into a ring which he believed to be of German origin; but then, again, he knew Rymer was capable of pulling off many things where a man of lesser mental calibre would have failed.

And Blake's instinct was right. If he had known something of Rymer's activities during the past few months the affair would have been crystal clear to him.

From the moment when he had discovered that the Jules Felibert whom he had rescued at Yokohama was the same wealthy Jules Felibert who had been making a tour of the Far East, Rymer's attentions had been entirely concentrated on just one thing—to win the Frenchman's gratitude to such an extent that he could improve his opportunities through it.

Nor had the Frenchman been niggardly. By the time the Andre Lebon reached Hong Kong he had again and again protested his deep gratitude for that which Rymer had done, and, aside from the purely selfish element of it, there could be no question that Rymer had indeed rescued him from what would have been certain death.

Thus it can be imagined what the Frenchman's feelings were when Rymer performed a double service in operating.

Felibert was a very wealthy man, and on the evening before the ship made Hong Kong he had a long talk with Rymer, during the course of which he made tentative suggestions that he would like to show, in some material way, the gratitude he felt.

Rymer was not precipitate. At first he brushed the suggestion aside, but not so definitely that he did not leave a loophole through which he could bring the subject of the concession in Korea.

A little to his surprise he found that Felibert knew all about the concession during the time it was under German development, and, while he would not join with Rymer in forming a new company, he did "persuade" the latter to accept a draft on Paris for no less than a hundred thousand francs.

Rymer was jubilant. With that much working capital in his pocket he figured he could swing something big out of it. At Hong Kong he left the Andre Lebon, which proceeded on to Haiphong and Saigon, and, after installing himself at the Hong Kong Hotel, Rymer's first business was to find out just what Germans were in the place at the time. It did not take him long to locate them, and he was elated when he discovered that one of them was a former member of the company that had opened up the Concession before the War.

This individual and Rymer soon became as thick as thieves, and just a week later Rymer sailed for Europe, bearing with him several letters of introduction to the chief financial interests in Berlin who had controlled the original concession.

Three weeks in Berlin was enough.

The German ring was already at work trying to figure out some way by which they could regain control of the concession, and their agents had already reported that there was a chance, owing to the differences in Korea between the Japs, the Chinese, the Koreans themselves, and the intriguing Bolshevists. They knew all about the tenders called for by the Japanese Government, but they never in their wildest dreams expected the actual concession to be offered to them.

Their nationality didn't matter to Rymer. He saw a chance to make the biggest clean-up he had ever had a chance at, and he was determined to put it through if possible. With the actual papers in his possession, and only needing the name of a company inserted to make them legal, he could pretty well dictate his own terms to the German crowd, and he did. They surrendered, and immediately a syndicate was formed to develop the property.

Things were rushed at high speed, and in less than a fortnight Rymer, as director in the Far East, left for Korea, accompanied by more than a hundred engineers and experts of various sorts. And he took good care that the actual documents of concession went with him.

He had almost unlimited drawing powers on Berlin, and as soon as he arrived in Korea he made deep inroads into these funds in order to buy up anyone who showed an inclination to baulk his plans.

The result was that, by the time Sexton Blake arrived on the scene, things were moving along smoothly at the concession, which was some sixty miles beyond Seul, and Rymer felt that at last he was going to make the one big clean-up he had always tried for.

But his co-directors in Germany were not so short-sighted as not to anticipate obstruction and prepare to meet it. It did not take them long to discover the activities of Mr. Algernon Birkmire and Baron Tayashi in London and Tokio, and one of their spies informed them of the visit of the pair to Sexton Blake less than two hours after they had left Baker Street. From that moment Blake and Tinker were under surveillance, and by the time the big junk slipped out of Kowloon, with Blake and Tinker on board, their movements had been pretty thoroughly covered.

That was why Rymer had come down from his luxurious quarters in Seul to remain in Chemulpo, on watch for the arrival of the junk. And that was why Blake had noticed a small, rusty tramp steaming up and down in erratic manner just after he and Tinker managed to get ashore.

At the moment when Blake and Tinker passed, Rymer had not been informed of the wreck of the junk. His last information had reached him the preceding day. He knew a strange junk of Canton type with a canvas sail was off the Shantung coast, but that was all. It was not until later in the day that he heard of the wreck and the supposition that all hands on board had perished. It was then that he was to heave a sigh of relief at the thought that the Baker Street pair had at last been wiped out of existence.

In the meantime Blake and Tinker were shuffling steadily along towards a certain small stone house just behind the Cho-Sen Hotel. On reaching their destination Blake knocked lightly on the closed door. There was a brief wait, and then the door was opened by a poorly-clad Japanese servant.

"Your master is at home?" said Blake curtly, adding a single word of apparently no meaning.

The servant had eyed them with some apprehension at first, but as he heard the single word he drew the door wider, and Blake and Tinker slipped inside. The man then opened a small door on the right, and they entered a meagrely-furnished room, where a stout, elderly

Japanese, clad little better than his servant, was seated cross-legged, evidently absorbed in a book. He looked up as they entered, and once again Blake uttered the single word that seemed to be an open sesame to the house.

He came to his feet swiftly, and, with a wave of the hand, dismissed the servant. As the door closed he shook hands, European fashion, with first Blake then Tinker.

"So you have come, Mr. Blake," he remarked. "I heard yesterday of the junk being off the coast, but I have been wondering if she survived the storm."

Blake shook his head the while he studied the man before him, a man who need not have lived in such austere surroundings but from his own desires, for Blake knew him to be wealthy in his own right, and one of Baron Tayashi's most trusted lieutenants.

The Japanese financier kept two confidential agents in Chemulpo and three in Seul, the second in Chemulpo being the other Japanese merchant to whom Blake had brought a letter.

By moving in both the upper and lower strata of the life of the place, the pair in Chemulpo, and the trio in Seul, were able to keep their fingers on the pulse of the intrigue-ridden country, and Blake knew that all they had been able to learn about the German crowd who had jumped the concession which rightly belonged to Anglo-Japanese interests, would be in his possession before night.

After a few words in which he described how the junk had been driven ashore and wrecked, and how he and Tinker had managed to reach the land safely, he felt beneath his shirt, and, unbuttoning one pocket of his belt, took out the letter which he had brought with him. He handed it across to the Jap, who merely said:

"It will be in the hands of my honoured colleague in less than half an hour, Mr. Blake. And while we are waiting, we shall take some refreshment, for I am sure both you and your young assistant must be badly in need of nourishment."

Blake did not deny the fact, and when their host had summoned the servant and had given him instructions about the letter, another servant was called and ordered to prepare food. Over the meal they discussed the business of the concession at length, and Blake picked up a good deal of valuable information. When the Jap had finished, and the cigarettes were going, Blake said:

"There is a big bearded man staying, I believe, at the Cho-Sen

Hotel, honourable one. I know something of this man. It is possible that he is not using the name that rightfully belongs to him. But I am wondering if by chance he has any connection with the interests that have taken over the concession. It is the type of thing he would be mixed up in if the chance came his way."

"I cannot tell you if that is so," answered the other. "That phase of the matter would be in the hands of my honourable colleague. We shall ask him when he comes."

Scarcely had he finished speaking when they heard the sound of a door being closed, and, a few seconds later, a prosperous-looking Japanese gentleman entered the room. He greeted his friend first, then he turned and shook hands with Blake and Tinker.

"Your disguises are perfection," he said, speaking, like his colleague, in almost unaccented English. "I have just been informed that the strange junk which was off Chemulpo yesterday perished in the storm. I had some fear that you and your assistant may have perished with her."

Blake smiled and shook his head.

"I fear all the others were lost," he said. "But fortune was with us, for we managed to reach the shore."

Then, as the matter was very urgent, they settled down to discuss the business which had brought Blake to the country, and he was not greatly surprised when the merchant, Mr. Soto Yama, confirmed his suspicions about Huxton Rymer.

But Blake knew that Rymer himself must believe himself to be standing on solid ground, for the merchant informed him that he had come down from Seul a few days before, and was staying at the Cho-Sen Hotel under his own name of Rymer. Blake and Tinker exchanged glances but made no comment.

"Your suspicions are more than correct, Mr. Blake," said the merchant, "although I cannot guess how you knew this. Not only is he closely connected with the people who are working the concession, but he is, in fact, the chief director of its operations. Ever since we discovered this we have been making close investigations in Seul, here in Chemulpo, in Tokio, and in Yokohama. And, from the reports I have received, it would appear that it was this man Rymer who got possession of the green portfolio from the person of the special messenger who was taking it to London.

"You have, of course, received some information from his

Excellency, Baron Tayashi. But his Excellency did not know at the time you left London as much as we have been able to discover since. My theory is that this man, Rymer, was in Yokohama at the time of the earthquake. I know for a fact that he sailed from that port on the French steamer Andre Lebon, and left the ship at Hong Kong.

"In Hong Kong he was in close association with German agents there, and it is a significant fact that on leaving Hong Kong, he proceeded direct to Europe and on to Berlin. In Berlin he had many interviews with the same financial people who had possession of the concession before the war. Then he came out to Korea, and with him came the vanguard of the German specialists who are now on the concession."

Blake smoked in thoughtful silence for some minutes before replying. Then he said:

"What you say is most interesting, Mr. Soto Yama, and dovetails perfectly with what I know of the man. I have an intimate knowledge of his doings for some years past, and such a thing as this concession is exactly what he would jump at. But I also know that, no matter what agreement he reached with the financial crowd in Berlin, he would never permit the master card to leave his own possession until he had cashed in to the extent which he had planned."

"You mean, Mr. Blake?"

"I mean simply that if he got possession of the green portfolio containing the documents relating to the concession, then those documents will still be under his personal control, if not actually in his possession."

"Then what do you propose?"

"He is staying at the Cho-Sen Hotel. When we saw him this morning he was in the act of leaving in a rickshaw. He may have intended to be gone for only a few minutes, or for some time. I take it there would not be much difficulty in one of your men gaining access to the room and making a careful inventory of the pieces of luggage he has with him?"

"None at all. Half a dozen of the servants there are our men."

"In that case it will be simple. If you could arrange to have that done, then I think I may be able to enlarge on the germ of a plan that is already in my mind. We must not forget that, just as we have discovered a good deal about him, he, in his turn, may have known that I was bound for Korea.

"In that case, he will be on guard and suspicious of everything at all out of the normal. And if his information is sufficient to convince him that I have actually arrived, then our job is going to be most difficult. He is a man of big mental calibre; it will take all our finesse to outwit him. In addition, we must act swiftly if we are to succeed—this very day if possible."

"What is your intention?"

"That is easily explained. Our job is to get hold of those documents before he places them out of our reach. On their possession rests the success or failure of my mission. Therefore, the sooner you can let me have the information I require, the more quickly can I round out my plan of action."

"The information you have asked for will be in your hands inside an hour, Mr. Blake," said the merchant briskly. "I myself shall bring it to you."

With that he rose, and, after shaking hands once more, took his leave. Following that, Blake and Tinker were given a room by their host, where they could lie down and take some badly needed rest.

Tinker soon dropped into a doze, but Blake sat smoking his yellow cigarettes, thinking, thinking, thinking, as he tried to figure out some way to outwit Huxton Rymer.

For no one knew better than Sexton Blake that quick and direct action was his only hope.

IT was about six o'clock in the evening when Mr. Soto Yama returned. Blake and Tinker had just finished tea when the merchant was shown in, and as soon as the usual format Eastern greetings were over, the latter plunged at once into the subject which was engaging all of them.

"I have succeeded in gaining the information you desire, Mr. Blake," he said. "Here is a sheet of paper on which you will find a detailed list of every visible object in the room of the man at the hotel."

Blake nodded and took the slip of paper. He glanced down the list, reading item after item, until his gaze paused at one which was: "One black, steel despatch-box, measuring sixteen English inches in length, ten English inches in depth, and eight English inches in width."

He nodded his head slightly at this item, then continued his perusal until again his eyes came to rest on another item almost at the end of the list. It read: "One steel box, such as is used in India and the Far East by British officers and other British travellers, measurements being four English feet in length, one English foot in depth, and two English feet in width."

Those two items alone seemed to hold Blake's attention, and, after conning the very last item, he looked up.

"There are two things here which I look upon as possibilities, Mr. Soto Yama," he said. "One is the steel despatch-box, and the other a steel uniform trunk. If our man has those documents in his possession, it is a good chance that they are locked up in one of the objects mentioned, providing he does not carry them on his person. I am inclined to believe he would take a chance like that.

"We may safely assume that the German financial group agreed to work with him, and at his terms, when they discovered he held the trump card; but, on the other hand, knowing that race, as I do, I fancy they are as anxious as we are to get the papers away from him. Therefore, Huxton Rymer would scarcely be likely to give them an opportunity of doing so by assaulting him when he was abroad alone.

"At any rate, in my opinion, the thing I have planned is worth trying. And if you can bring me what I now require in addition, my assistant and I shall make the attempt."

"What else is it you require, Mr. Blake?"

"I require impressions of the locks taken and keys made to fit them."

"That will not be easy."

"Could it not be arranged while he was at dinner?"

The merchant rubbed his chin thoughtfully. Then:

"Nothing must be impossible in this business. What time shall you want the keys?"

"Not later than eleven to-night."

"Then rest easy, Mr. Blake. At eleven o'clock to-night the keys you wish will be in your hands."

"Good!" And Blake did not ask how it would be arranged. Then he added: "I propose paying a visit to the man's room after that hour. He may or may not be there at the time, I shall be prepared for either. Can you let ne have a couple of men who can get us into the grounds at the back of the hotel without our being seen? Then I must have the exact location of the room pointed out to me."

"It is at the back overlooking the garden. I can, of course, supply any number of trust-worthy men,"

"Two will be sufficient. It helps things that the room is at the back. Please instruct one of the men carefully just which one it is, so that he can point it out to me. We can't afford to make any mistakes. And, incidentally, it would be well if they could smuggle into the garden a bamboo ladder."

"All shall be exactly as you wish, Mr. Blake. As for me, I shall come here it eleven with the two men and the keys. Then I shall wait until you return from your precarious expedition. As soon is it is quite dark I shall have a ladder quietly smuggled into the garden as you request."

With that the merchant once more took his departure, and, since they could do no more until his return, Blake and Tinker again lay down, for they knew not what that night might bring forth.

At exactly eleven the merchant returned. He slipped into the little stone house quietly and entered the room where Blake and Tinker lay, like a shadow. He had doffed his European clothes, and was now clad in the dress of his native land, and his movements were as noiseless as those of a cat.

"I have the keys," he whispered, "and I shall myself go with you. My two men are waiting outside. All is ready to get into the garden, and the ladder is already concealed there. Our man is still sitting in the lounge playing cards with three other Europeans."

Blake and Tinker got to their feet.

"How are your weapons?" went on the Jap. "In case yours were damaged in the wreck, I can supply you with others."

"Ours are all right," whispered Blake. "We have gone over them very carefully, and have plenty of ammunition. We shall go at once."

The three figures, one in the garb of a Jap and the other two still in their coolie garments, left the room and passed out to the street. As they emerged, two shadowy figures detached themselves from the darkness and proceeded just ahead of them.

The garden of the Cho-Sen Hotel was only a stone's-throw away, and inside five minutes they were over the wall.

While the two men the merchant had brought along with him stole off to get the bamboo ladder which they had hidden, the merchant led the way along between the dense bushes until they emerged just under a window at the eastern corner of the hotel. He touched Blake's arm and pointed upwards.

"That is the room," he whispered. "I would like to go up with you."

"No," answered Blake swiftly. "It would be better if you remained here with the two men on guard. I shall take only my assistant. He and I have done this sort of work before, and he knows just what I want him to do. We can work much more quickly than if there are three of us."

"Very well," agreed the Jap.

At that moment there was a soft, almost imperceptible, rustle in the bushes close to them, and an instant later the pair who had gone to get the ladder appeared. At a word from their master they placed it against the wall just under the window which was Blake's objective.

Before mounting Blake drew out his automatic pistol and stuck it in the waistband of his loose cotton garment, where he could get at it swiftly if necessary. Tinker followed suit. Next, Blake took out from under his shirt a small electric torch, and for an instant there was a flash while the merchant drew out the keys and indicated which one would fit the steel trunk and which the despatch-box.

Blake handed the former to Tinker, and himself kept possession of the other. Then, with a whispered word to the lad, he began to mount the ladder. Tinker followed close after, and when he saw

Blake's shadowy form suddenly disappear from view, he knew that the window of the room had been left open against the warm spring night air.

Tinker crawled into the room, and felt his way along until he saw a flash of the torch. He drew out his own, and followed Blake's example, and as he joined the latter he saw what Blake had already spotted. The steel trunk had been pushed under the bed, while the despatch-box was on a teak table close to it. Blake bent close to Tinker's ear and whispered:

"Pull the trunk out as softly as possible, then get busy. I'll attend to the despatch-box. You know what to look for—a green portfolio."

With his light in one hand, Tinker set to work while Blake gave his attention to the despatch-box. There had been no shoddy work about getting those duplicate keys made, for in each case they fitted as easily as if made by the firm which had manufactured the boxes.

As he lifted the lid of the despatch-box Blake saw that it was almost full of papers and documents of various kinds. He wasted little time on these, and began to probe for the object he sought. He was still thus engaged when he heard a soft hiss behind him, and, turning his head, saw that Tinker was squatting on his heels holding up a soiled green leather portfolio.

Blake bent swiftly and opened it. It took him less than ten seconds to assure himself that the actual papers he was after were inside. The honours were to Tinker, and as he closed it he motioned for the lad to put the portfolio inside his shirt.

"Lock the trunk, push it back, and then get out," he whispered. "I'll lock up the despatch-box and follow."

He turned back to replace the papers he had taken from the despatch-box, but he could hear the lock of the trunk click, and a soft scraping sound as Tinker pushed it back under the bed. Then there came a soft padding of feet as the lad obeyed orders and made for the window. Blake thrust in the last paper, and, locking the despatch-box, had just turned, and could see Tinker's silhouette against the open window, when the door suddenly flew open, and the next instant the room was flooded with light as the switch was turned on. Blake turned his head like a flash, and found himself gazing upon Rymer himself —Rymer in full evening dress, with a heavy blue automatic gleaming dully against the immaculate white of his dress shirt. Out of the corner of his eye he could see Tinker in a hesitating position on the very edge of the window. As he saw Rymer's wrist stiffen, Blake knew that the adventurer was going to shoot first, and ask questions after.

He flung himself to one side, clawing for his own weapon, calling at the same time:

"Out with you, my lad! Leave this to me!"

The last words were lost as Rymer's heavy pistol spoke once, twice, and again, and twice Blake felt the bullets brush his very cheek as he flung first to this side, then to that. He was almost flat on the floor as he pumped his own automatic, and he knew he had struck home with at least one bullet, for he saw Rymer's white shirt begin to grow crimson as a stain appeared up near the collar.

But apparently it was not serious, for Rymer gave vent to a curse and flung himself forward to come to closer quarters. At that instant there was a rapid rattle of another weapon as Tinker began shooting from the window, and under the spray of lead which he was pumping from his automatic the three electric bulbs in the chandelier were smashed to atoms, leaving the room in darkness.

Blake lost no time in taking advantage of this. He flung himself clean across the bed, and, with another shout to Tinker, turned to meet Rymer. The latter had paused to take a pot shot at Tinker, but the lad had slipped from the sill and was half-way to the ground by that time. Blake fired at the flash, but could not tell if he had found his mark for Rymer made no sound.

Blake's objective was, of course, the window. But he knew that he had no chance of getting through that way, for, while Rymer was standing waiting, he could easily pick off Blake before the latter could get clear.

Not that Blake funked coming to close grips with Rymer. On the contrary. Many, many times in the past those two men had tested each other's strength, endurance, and courage, and up to date the percentage of victories was certainly substantially in Blake's favour.

But at the present time Blake had every reason for getting away without further complications arising. He had, he believed, secured that for which he had travelled all the way from England, and his only desire now was to complete the business as soon as possible.

There was no criminal charge to be made against Rymer. If it could have been proved that it was actually he who had taken the green portfolio from the messenger, then the Japanese authorities might have made some sort of a case of it.

But the messenger, being dead, could not be produced as a material witness, and after that terrible welter of confusion which had followed the appalling events in Tokio and Yokohama, the Government had far too much to do to give its attention to the complaint of a group of foreign capitalists.

If the Anglo-Japanese group could actually produce the documents in question, then new tenders would be called for, and it was a safe bet that a new concession would be given to the group for which Blake was acting. That was his end of the affair, and now that Tinker had apparently got safely away with the prize he was not anxious to have any delay.

But the decision was taken out of Blake's hands. Rymer was evidently not disposed to allow the precious documents to be lifted without making a supreme effort to retake them. Of course, he was assuming that it was Blake himself who had them on his person.

There was no doubt in his mind now that the two "coolies" whom he had surprised in his room were the Baker Street pair. His information that afternoon had been that the strange junk had perished with all hands, but a single second after entering his room he knew that his information had been at fault.

He shot twice more at random; then, as Blake replied once, Rymer came plunging across the room, and before Blake could dodge him, the two had crashed together. In the past they had fought in every conceivable fashion, and each knew something of the other's tricks. But on this occasion there was no standing up knee to knee and hitting out.

It would have been impossible to see in that dark room, and every blow would have been at random. Instead, they were interlocked in deadly embrace, and as muscle tightened against muscle and leg stiffened against leg, they braced in silence, each ready for the slightest weakening on the part of his antagonist.

Suddenly the bright flash of an electric torch caused both men to shift involuntarily, but Blake was the first to recover, and as the light gleamed steadily upon them, and he heard Tinker's voice at the window, he managed to drag himself clear and drive his right hard to the body, following it swiftly with a sharp left jab to the jaw.

Rymer rocked back.

There was nothing else he could do under the impact of what was behind those blows. But he recovered himself quickly, and, with both fists driving like battering rams, he sent in a shower of terrific body blows which, despite his defence, drove Blake back.

Blake covered up, and remained on the defence until he had jockeyed his way close to the window; then, gathering himself together, he sprang in during a fleeting second in which Rymer left himself uncovered, and with a hard right to the solar plexus, followed by a terrific left to the point of the jaw, he handed out all he had.

A Dempsey might have weathered those two blows. Old Bob Fitzsimmons might have come back with that terrible right of his dealing out vengeance. Jim Jeffries might have grunted as used to be his wont, and mustered up a grin. But Rymer, while a husky and really magnificent fighter, was not a professional heavy-weight, and, just as surely as if he had taken chloroform, did those two well-timed and beautifully placed blows put him to sleep.

He rocked for a second, then he went down with a crash. There was a convulsive movement as some spirit within him urged him to rise, but the next moment that same spirit was swept along into the "never-never" land, where nothing matters, and as a hammering at the door followed, Blake staggered towards the window and thrust his feet out to feel for the ladder.

Tinker was about half-way down, and as Blake reached the ground after him, he said:

"I could have slugged him 'too easy,' guv'nor, but I knew you'd give me gippo if I did, so I let it go on."

Blake grunted his agreement; then, with a sign to the Japanese merchant, he intimated that he wanted to get away as quickly as possible. They stole back the way they had come, and, once over the wall, made for the little stone house which they had made their headquarters. There, by the light of a paper lantern, they were able to make a detailed examination of the contents of the green portfolio, and Mr. Soto Yama was able to identify the documents as complete in series, and exactly what they had been seeking.

The disguised Blake turned like a flash, and found himself gazing at Huxton Rymer—Rymer in full evening dress, with a heavy, blue automatic gleaming dully against the white of his dress shirt. (*Chapter 7.*)

THE following day, Blake, in a complete outfit supplied by the British Consul in Chemulpo, and Tinker clad in a suit supplied by a broad-shouldered young assistant in Mr. Soto Yama's employ who had been educated in England, and had brought out a plentiful supply of London-made clothes with him, entered the Cho-Sen Hotel and sauntered through the palm court on their way to the dining-room.

Mr. Soto Yama was host, and that all-powerful gentleman had taken the precaution to reserve a corner table, and to order the best tiffin the hotel chef could provide.

The details of the documents had been all settled. That same afternoon Blake and Tinker were to leave for Hong Kong in a small but well-fitted steamer belonging to the Tayashi Kaisha Line, and with Blake would go the papers, which he was to hand personally to Mr. Algernon Birkmire and Baron Tayashi in London.

From what the merchant had been able to tell them, the manager of the hotel had been unable to get from Rymer any explanation of the commotion in his room the previous night, and from that Blake deduced that the adventurer had made up his mind that he would gain nothing by "squealing."

Nor was Blake surprised when, as they walked the full length of the dining-room, he passed a table about half-way down, and Rymer, immaculately clad as usual, was nonchalantly eating his luncheon as if nothing had happened to ruffle his equanimity.

Blake smiled a trifle as he passed, and the two enemies bowed as any two casual acquaintances might have saluted each other. Tinker's smile was more a grin of triumph, but Rymer nodded coolly enough, and went on with his lunch. Blake and the other two were still at the table when Rymer lit a cigar and strolled out, but Blake made no comment—then.

At exactly four o'clock that afternoon the Baker Street pair got away. The ship was being sent to Hong Kong as a special for them, and hence they had the whole of the passenger accommodation to themselves, which, considering their experience in the junk, was welcome enough.

There was no sign of the fury of the recent storm that evening. The yellow sea had even lost its saffron ugliness under the slanting rays of the warm spring sun. Here and there crazy-looking junks were wallowing along in the leisurely manner of the East, and once a snow-white yacht sped by on its way to Port Arthur, or perhaps Tsein-tsin.

About two miles out of Chemulpo, when Blake and Tinker were pacing the after-deck, talking of the events of the past weeks, they saw a grey-painted boat of the Canton Line making port. As he spied it, Blake pointed towards it and said:

"I shouldn't mind making a mild wager, my lad, that when that steamer clears from Chemulpo our friend Rymer will be found among her passengers."

Tinker grinned.

"And I'll bet, guv'nor, that if he is, he takes with him a good slice of the funds belonging to the German gang on the concession."

Which was a truer prophecy than the lad guessed, for Rymer did leave Korea by that ship, and with him went every yen to the credit of the German group in the Chemulpo banks, and nearly the whole credit balance in Seul which he had had collected by telegram from Chemulpo.

Rymer's big scheme had been nipped in the bud, but as he, too, stood, a couple of days later, gazing back at the receding town which he had left in such haste, he was not entirely dissatisfied.

"It might have been worse," he muttered, as he chewed the end of his cigar. "Two years of a clear run and I'd have cleaned up close to a million before that gang of Boches got wise. But with my drafts and cash I've cleaned up a hundred thousand sterling, which is enough to keep the wheels greased for a time, at least." Then his eyes grew savage. "And, by Heaven, it's enough to enable me to lie low until I can figure out some scheme to 'get' Sexton Blake. Get him I will, and this time it will be for keeps."

But that threat would not have disturbed Sexton Blake's peace of mind in the least degree. He was perfectly satisfied with his journey to the East. He had a two-fold purpose to achieve, and he had succeeded.

Not only had he secured the documents vital to the interests of his clients, but he had beaten one of the cleverest crooks at large at his own game, and, as Tinker remarked, there was a jolly fat fee waiting for them when they should reach London.

But in that Blake had far less interest than in the thought that once again the entry in the famous "Index" at Baker Street would mark a triumph, and not a failure.

As for the German crew on the concession, it was a very

bedraggled and hangdog lot that reached Chemulpo some three weeks later. At that port there was a ship waiting to transport them back to their Fatherland, and the efficient Mr. Soto Yama was right on the job to see that not one was left behind.

What their reception was on their arrival in Berlin is of little interest, for we all know how the Boche treats the man who fails to make good. But with the documents which Sexton Blake brought back with him to prove their case, the Anglo-Japanese Development Company was able to take formal possession of the concession, and in the safe at Baker Street there are to-day quite a nice little bundle of preference bonds in that undertaking which promise to add materially to Blake's fortunes and Tinker's savings.

Which, as Tinker says, is a "bit of all right!"

THE END.
[20700 WORDS]

The TRUTH about CAPTAIN KIDD

What he was; what he did; and how he did it! No flights of fancy just pure, historical fact! The real life-story of this famous pirate will appear in next week's Supplement — and the following weeks! This is a series feature of surpassing interest. Illustrated by "Val." Watch out for—

The TRUTH about CAPTAIN KIDD

The Atom Smasher

By L. H. Robbins

A Story of the Years to Come— And of the Power of the Atom.

THE FIRST CHAPTERS.

AMERICA, in the year 1940, is in the grip of two gigantic forces. One is a vast revolutionary organisation of militant industrial terrorists, calling themselves the "Red Eyes," or "Irresistibles," and the other is the newly discovered power of the Atom— the result of years of research, in which the scientists of our own day are even now engaged.

A man thought to be Colonel Allan Derwin is killed in an explosion attributed to the "Red Eyes." Paul Mercer, a young newspaperman, discovers that the dead man is not Derwin, but an impostor killed in mistake.

The colonel, the "big" man in American finance, desires to keep his continued existence a secret, and asks Paul to help him in his plans for frustrating the designs of the "Red Eyes." Paul does so, and resigns from his paper, "The Blaze."

Paul takes Derwin's wife and his daughter Nalla to the safety of the colonel's country home. On the way in the car they find a workman being attacked by a number of others.

Paul rescues him, and Nalla, giving him her card, promises to hold him if necessary. The man leaves them, and later the car is held up by another party in search of him, but without success.

The party arrives in safety at Colonel Derwin's country house, and, in spite of being tempted to stay, Paul determines to go back to the city after a few hours' sleep, although there will be a grave danger in doing so.

(Now *read on.*)

Tempted!

AWAKING at noon from a sleep miles deep, and looking from his window across the sunny lawns of the Derwin domain, Mercer in great dejection almost repented his stern resolution of the night.

Someone, while he slept, had supplied him with shaving materials and fresh linen—he could guess who. As he finished dressing, a servant brought word from Nalla that breakfast awaited his pleasure.

A table for two was set on a side piazza. Nalla at the coffee-urn delighted his eyes.

"Do you still mean to go back to town?" she asked.

"Yep." he answered, between bites of toast, "I don't suppose I can do much good, though. Your father has the whole Metals staff at his command. But I can at least be hanging around when the story breaks. It will make me solid with dear Mr. Hicks again."

"Who is he?"

"My City editor."

"Is he personally responsible for everything his newspaper prints?"

"For all the City news, yes."

"For the Society news, for instance?"

"Surely. Why?"

"I just wondered."

Again it occurred to Mercer that she didn't approve of his newspaper. But she withheld further comment in that direction, perhaps out of regard for his feelings.

"You speak of papa's having his Metals organisation to help him," she said. "That isn't quite true, for he intends to make the fight practically alone. Besides us here, only Lambeth Dunn and Mr. Duguid and Mr. Pardee are to know the truth, that he is still alive."

"The more reason, then, why I should be where things are doing. A man as big as your father can't keep such a secret very long. If he gets away with his plan there will have to be quick work."

"That's so," she admitted, and held out her lovely though unadorned left hand for his coffee-cup, her right being engaged in regulating the flame under the urn.

She was very kind to him that morning, as she was kind to everybody always. Her last thoughtful attention, before accompanying him to the wharf to see him ferried out to the White Curlew, was to hunt up a sweater and make him put it on under his leather coat.

Giles was already on board the flying-boat; he was a lank, taciturn fellow with eyes as cool and hands as steady as steel.

"Make yourself comfortable," he bade his passenger, as he set the engines humming.

Away from the shore the Curlew taxied and took position facing the west wind. The engines changed their tune from a croon to a full-throated anthem.

Mercer, looking back, saw Nalla wave her left hand in farewell as the wings caught the air.

The Council of War.

FROM Pelham Bay, the home port of the White Curlew, Mercer journeyed by subway to the Seventies and walked toward the park. In the dusk he saw that the Derwin house had been boarded up since the previous day. Blank and apparently tenant-less, it faced the Avenue as in midsummer.

Around the corner, in the side-street, he paused before the iron gate and pressed an electric button. He heard a door open somewhere in the shadows, and a man came towards him,

"Bolby?"

"Oh! It's you, Mr. Mercer. I quite failed to recognise you in your chauffeur togs. I've saved your other clothes for you upstairs, sir."

The butler unlocked the gate, admitted the young man, locked it again, and led the way into the house.

"You're to step right up, sir—the door to your left at the head of the stairs."

Mercer tapped at the door of a room within which were lights and voices.

Allan Derwin greeted him, rising from a table at which three other men were seated.

"Glad to see you, Paul. Nalla has told me what a good driver you are. Do you know these gentlemen—Mr. Duguid, Mr. Dunn, Mr. Pardee?"

The brisk Lambeth Dunn reached across the table with a quick hand. Stout Campbell Duguid nodded. The weazened banker, Pardee, said, with a wink:

"You didn't stay north long, young man. New England not attractive this time of year?"

"Business before pleasure," Mercer laughed. "Have we spiked the atomic gun yet?"

Derwin sat down and motioned the newcomer to a chair nearby. On the table a blue print was spread an architect's picture of a city street. Mercer saw that the structure represented in the middle of the drawing was the American Metals Building.

"We have been interested," the colonel explained, "in this sketch that Mr. Dunn had made for us this afternoon. It shows, as you see, our headquarters, with the Pinchon Building on the right and the International Zinc Building across Broadway on the left."

With a pencil Mr. Derwin pointed.

"Here is my office. About here would be my desk."

He enlarged the pencil dot that already marked the spot.

"Down here on the right, under the side-walk level, are, or were, the Pinchon boilers."

He made another dot, then slid a ruler into such position that the brass edges rested upon the two marks. The upper end of the ruler lay across the Zinc Building.

"The fourth, fifth, and sixth stories of the Zinc Building are used as offices by the Allied Zinc Companies. A straight line from the heart of the Pinchon boiler-room through my office cuts the Zinc-Building at the fifth story. Since the Zinc Building completely fills that side of the street, there being no alley along-side it, we have assumed that the thoughtful person who tried to assassinate me yesterday did his work from a window in the Allied Zinc offices."

"You believe, sir, that the death of the man at your desk and the explosion of the boilers were due to the same cause?"

"After what I saw on the Elizabeth meadows the day before yesterday I can't think anything else. The boiler explosion was probably a side incident that wasn't intended to happen."

"The office rooms facing Broadway on the fifth floor of the Zinc Building," observed Mr. Duguid, "are used by the president of the Allied Companies, our friend Jules Manton."

Mercer whistled.

"But Manton is one of your crowd. He is one of the men you took into your confidence."

"He was with us when we first talked over the inventor's proposition," said Pardee, "but not when we decided to reject it. Why wasn't he here, Derwin, when you told us about the mail plane?"

"Because I didn't invite him. If you recall, he was in favour of looking into the invention. He rather fancied it as a weapon that would give us an awful advantage against our enemies. So I didn't ask him into our consultations again."

"You did the right thing!" Pardee snapped, and Duguid added:

"He's out of date, old style, no love for his fellow-men, no faith in 'em. If he had his way he would keep labour and capital at odds for the rest of eternity. He has a lot to learn."

"Have you shown him this diagram?" inked Mercer.

"Unfortunately," Lambeth Dunn answered, "Jules Manton has disappeared. That's where you may be able to help us."

Derwin raised a warning hand. In the hush a man's voice, gruff and excited, was heard from the floor below.

"Manton himself!" muttered Pardee, and Mr. Dunn added grimly:

"I guess we sha'n't need the young man for that job, after all."

They heard Bolby speaking.

"The first door to your left, sir, at the head of the stairs. You'll find Mr. Pardee there, sir."

Silence outside, then a knock.

"Come in!" the little banker called. Before them stood Jules Manton, broad-shouldered, dark, sullen, and anxious.

"Come in, Manton! We're all friends here," spoke Pardee.

But Manton clung to the door with one hand and reached towards Colonel Derwin with the other as if to ward off an evil spirit.

"Allan Derwin!" His lips moved; his voice failed.

Lambeth Dunn had circled the table in time to catch the big man as he reeled. Safe in a chair, the zinc man still stared at Derwin, nerve-shaken, dumbfounded, gulping at last:

"You're—you're not dead?"

"No, Manton," his host replied. "I'm still alive and able to see company. I'm glad you dropped in."

"So—so am I," the zinc man stammered. "So am I, although I didn't drop in. You gentlemen know that."

"We were sorry to use force in bringing you here," said Pardee. "But we had to have you. We'd like you to tell us about the attempt on Derwin's life that was made from your office yesterday morning."

Manton sat crumpled, his big hands gripping the chair arms. Still he stared at the man he had believed to be dead.

"If Derwin is alive, then who the devil was—"

"A double—a crook, we think," Pardee answered. "But that's of little importance now. The fact remains that the bolt or blow or flash, or whatever it was that killed him came from your rooms on the fifth floor of the Zinc Building."

"How you know that is too much for me," Manton replied, "unless the murderer himself told you. But I—I can't believe— I'm so glad it wasn't Derwin. You'll have to excuse me, gentlemen, but I can't help this."

He had quite broken down. His face twitched and wrinkled. He wept like a great child, as Mercer had seen an exhausted football captain weep at the close of a terrific game.

"We know you are glad," said Lambeth Dunn. "Meanwhile, time gallops. So come across; let's hear your story."

Thus adjured, Jules Manton pulled himself together, hulking, powerful as a bull, yet with averted eyes and halting words.

"When we talked the day before yesterday about that atomic gun, I knew that you all were against it. You didn't see the possibilities in the thing for us if we could get it and keep it our own for use in fighting the blackguard Red Eyes.

"In our meeting in Derwin's office I expressed my views. You didn't warm up to them. If you wanted the invention at all, you wanted it not because it might become a weapon for us, but because it might contain a world-beating scientific discovery that could be used in industry."

"A new source of mechanical power, precisely!" Derwin commented.

"I knew then that it was thumbs down, with you all. I guessed that Derwin would not keep that nine o'clock appointment at Grand Central, no matter what miracle he might see the thing perform on the salt meadows. So I kept the date in his stead."

"You did, as we know," said Pardee. "We had a few of our people there on the chance of spotting anybody who seemed to be looking for Derwin. They saw you and reported the fact to us. But you met no one."

Manton showed no surprise.

"At nine o'clock sharp." he continued, "I called at the information booth for a Michigan Central time-table, then sat down near the waiting-room door, with the time-table in plain sight. I sat there till half-past ten. In the hour and a half I was looked over by three men and a woman to my knowledge."

"Could you identify them if you saw them again?"

"All but the woman. She was veiled. There's no need to tell you how I know that these people studied me. I simply knew it, that's all; and the thing that happened next morning proves that I'm at least partly right. At least, one of the four was there as a scout for the people who've been writing to Derwin.

"I didn't go home to Tarrytown that night. I went to the Kremlin Hotel, registered by a name that I use when I don't want to be conspicuous, and got a room. At half-past three in the morning the phone bell in my room woke me up.

"The hotel operator spoke to me, using the name I had written in the book, and explained that he wouldn't have called me if he had not been assured that the call was a message from my family and of great importance. Then he put the call on, and a woman's voice asked me if I was Mr. Manton. Thinking it was Tarrytown on the wire I answered, 'Yes.'

" 'You change your name so readily,' said the woman, 'I scarcely know what to call you. But it shall be Manton if you like, Mr. Manton.' Her voice was a contralto, young and cheerful. I thought at first it was someone having fun with me; but I got over that notion in a hurry, for she went on, speaking rapidly and not wasting words, and told me, in effect, this:

"That I was known to be associated with you, Mr. Derwin, in the management of the metals industries, and it was judged, from my appearance and behaviour at Grand Central, that I was aware of the proposition made to you, and was more interested in it than you were, since I had taken the trouble to keep the appointment arranged for you.

"Further, if I would pledge my honour as a gentleman that no trap would be laid, no leading questions asked, and no interference offered, and that strict confidence would be guaranteed, an agent representing the inventor of the atomic gun would call upon me at my office the following day at ten o'clock."

"You did not know then the particulars of the destroying of the mail plane above the Jersey meadows?" Colonel Derwin asked.

"I don't know them yet," Manton replied, "although I read of that affair, and wondered if there might not be some connection between it and your trip over there. Later in the day, after I had seen what the atomic gun did to you—or to the man I thought was you—then I could guess what happened to the plane."

"You gave the woman the appointment she asked for?"

"I did, gentlemen; and I think you all know I'm telling the truth when I say that my motive was nothing worse than mercenary.

"I had read a lot of prophecy about atomic energy, as I told you the other day. I knew a colossal discovery would come some time; something would be found that would close the coal mines and stop the oil-wells and revolutionise industry and transportation and life in general. I always thought of it in terms of fuel.

"Well, here it had come, and the chance was offered to me to get in on the ground floor, and I fell for it. I gave the woman all the guarantees she asked, and I agreed to meet her agent.

"All the while I promised myself to let you people in on the good thing. I would at least show you that there was no harm in looking it over. But I couldn't pass you the word until after my interview with the agent, having assured him of a confidential meeting at which no one else should be present.

"I had my plans made to send for you right away afterwards and prove to you that I was a better business man than any of you. But, of course, there's no good in telling you that part of it now.

"At ten o'clock I waited in my private office, having left word outside that I expected a strange caller. At ten sharp my caller came, and he was a strange one, for sure.

"He was a cross-eyed, wild-eyed man of fifty years or so, a wiry little man about the size of Pardee, and he had the hands and the neck and the skin of a man who has spent his life at manual labour. He was as full of business as a stick of dynamite. He began right off the reel by telling me he had me absolutely at his mercy.

"I took his opening remark as a pleasantry and asked him to have a chair. But he wouldn't sit down. He walked the floor, talking at a great rate, and stopping now and then to look out the windows. There are three windows in my room that face the Metals Building, as perhaps you know.

"He carried under his arm a blue leather box about as big as the city directory, there on the stand. Attached to the box was a steel chain, and the other end of the chain was padlocked to his wrist. He explained the chain. As long as he kept possession of the blue leather box he had nothing to fear from any man or any number of men.

" 'If you try to stop me from leaving when I get ready to go,' he told me, 'I will kill you, and after you every other man in my way! I will destroy this building, but I shall escape.'

(Who is the mysterious man with the blue leather box—and what is in the box? Next week's instalment will narrate what happened at Manton's interview with the Atom-Smasher—and its startling sequel. This is a yarn worth keeping in touch with!)

The UNIO

THE UNION JACK 2ᴰ

Sexton Blake's Own Paper

THE MUMMY'S TWIN
A Story of Prince Menes and Sexton Blake

PRINCE MENES

The Return of the " Man from Everywhere!"

Next week's yarn is a star turn in a succession of star turns. It features the reappearance of an old character long absent from the circle of Sexton Blake's opponents. It is, moreover, of especial interest in view of the recent sensational discoveries of Egyptian antiquities at Luxor. The yarn itself is a thriller. You will revel in it. Prince Menes is a character worth welcoming back. Be at the newsagent's early next Thursday with your twopence for

THE MUMMY'S TWIN.

Or, better still,
ORDER IT WHILE
THERE IS STILL
TIME!

www.ingramcontent.com/pod-product-compliance
Lightning Source LLC
Chambersburg PA
CBHW030328130626
46554CB00011B/1000